RETRIBUTION

DAVID HORN

ISBN: 978-1-959493-63-1 (sc)
ISBN: 978-1-959493-62-4 (ebk)

BOOK 1

SYNOPSIS

OVER THE WEEK-END OF JUNE 24th 1996 in the pleasant Victorian holiday town of Harrogate in Northern England three horrific murders were committed. Although similar, the police believed them to be unconnected. However, as this story unfolds it would seem that they were connected but not in the way it would seem. It would appear they were committed by three unassociated individuals.

- The first was a brilliant, beautiful student doctor about to become qualified. She had been savagely beaten, raped and then strangled.
  Vanessa Machin was 25 and a student doctor who was on the threshold of a medical career a beautiful girl, full of life and vitality. She was found raped and brutally bashed on Saturday morning under bushes near the Church of Christ on the stray (a large grass area in the town). Her injuries were so severe they shocked the detectives investigating.

- The second was a young Downs Syndrome girl with a pleasant, friendly nature. A funny looking Mongol, her face beaten beyond recognition, had chocked on her own blood and vomit.

Shirley Wilson was a Downs Syndrome girl; a dumpy girl so severely beaten she was unrecognizable; dumped near the river at Canal Road. This was the next victim found on Sunday morning. Her identity had to be sought by dental records.

- The third was an ordinary pretty young girl. The attractive 20 year old had been brutalized and raped, her injuries beyond belief.
  Helen Johnson was a shop assistant and like Vanessa was raped and beaten. She was found at Plumpton Rocks, a picnic spot on the Wetherby Road.

Each of these girls were found within half a mile of each other on three consecutive nights in the North Yorkshire town of Harrogate, a pleasant old town centred on the stray which was a large open grassed area left to the townsfolk by an ancient philanthropist. Not since the 'Yorkshire Ripper' had such brutality surfaced.

Harrogate Police had no precedence for murders like these as nothing like this had happened since the Yorkshire Ripper days 10 years earlier. But Peter Sutcliffe, the Yorkshire Ripper, was behind bars leaving them baffled. They could find no witnesses or connections between these three girls. Forensics in 1996 was not as sophisticated as it is today and they could find no clues as to who or why these crimes were committed.

* * * * * * * * * * * * * *

PREFACE

Clyde was Vanessa's twin brother, a colonel in the SAS; the youngest to ever reach colonel having achieved this before he was 25.

Using his extraordinary skills and the help of a past master of the United Grand Lodge of England he tracks down a mainland collector for the IRA (Sean McCracken) whom he believes killed his sister. Tracking him from Belfast to Libya, across the great Libyan Desert to the foothills of the black Africa. Believing he has avenged his sister's death he participates in the ancient warrior tournament held every 5 years by the decedents of the 5 families of Desert Arabs who ruled under King Iddress before Kaddafi seized power.

From Libya to a small village in Southern Ireland, where both 'The Hunter' and 'The Hunted' have their ancestral roots.

The fat man smiled, keeping his hand on Sean's head. Slowly but firmly the man then placed his other hand on the boys head and pushed him down towards his crutch – sticking out from his open trouser fly was an erect penis. Sean started to struggle but the fat man gripped his hair firmly with both hands and forced Sean's head down onto his penis. "Go on," he said, "suck this." Sean opened his mouth to scream but before any sound could escape the man forced his penis into the boy's mouth and moved his head backward and forward. "That's it. That's right, go on, suck it!" said the man as he began to move more vigorously.

Just then, something in Sean snapped, nobody had ever spoken to him about anything remotely like this, and he'd certainly not seen any of the farm animals do anything like this. He had known sex itself was powerful; he had already experienced several erections watching the farm animals mating; but this was different, wrong. Savagely, he bit the penis with his teeth, so violently in fact, nearly severing the head. The fat man screamed and let go of Sean's head, doubling over and screaming with shock and pain. Sean merely stood and stared down at the man with contempt. Sean now had the advantage; he was wearing hard leather farm boots with steel studs. Deliberately and carefully aimed, he kicked the man's head and watched him fall to his knees. Again and again he kicked the fat florid face until the man lay still, on his side, his damaged penis now limp, pumped bright red blood onto the cracked concrete floor. Sean had never felt like this before elated and flushed with excitement. The fat man was dead before Sean had even reached his uncle's new car. That was Sean's first murder.

* * * * * * * * * * * * * *

Jack was a rich and successful pharmacist and the father of the Downs Syndrome girl; his strange, lovely gentle daughter beaten to a pulp. Leading a double life, he discovers a deviant serving time in a local jail that he believes to be responsible for his daughters murder. By the time Jack is convinced he has found the right man, he has been released from jail and joined an all singing, all dancing praise the risen lord, born again now order Christian crusade in America lead by the homosexual Rev Algernon Godleman; the power behind the Assembly of God.

* * * * * * * * * * * * * *

Jack laid face down on the massage table. Belinda poured oil onto her hands and then rubbed them together. He closed his eyes as she slowly slid her oily hands over his shoulders, down his back, kneading and massaging each joint in his back, over his buttocks, down the cheeks, onto his inner thighs, down the back of his legs, kneading his calves and ankles, each leg in turn. Belinda knew her job. Back up she went, retracing the path her hands had made the first time, shoulders, neck............" OK Johnny, turn over now." He turned over and placed his hands behind his head. She looked at this flaccid penis as she poured more oil onto her hands. "That's no good," she said in mock disapproval, "no good at all. You're not concentrating. He's normally stood up by now."

Slowly she opened the buttons of her tunic down to her waist, her large firm breasts swinging out as she took off each shoulder and pulled out her arms. As the tunic fell around her ankles, she took off her small G-string. "That's more like it!" she said as he slowly began to get aroused. "Do you want ride-a-cock-hose today Johnny?" she asked. Jack nodded.

She threw a leg over the bed and sat, slowly, astride him. The massage table began to squeak as she did a ride-a-cock-horse. The music played 'Hey Jude' and then 'Green sleeves', the bed went squeakity scratch, scratchity squeak, faster and faster then slowed until it finally stopped. The music played 'The Green Green Grass of Home.'

* * * * * * * * * * * * * *

Mary was a staff sister at Harrogate General Hospital and never liked Terry. He was a psychopath; part-time office worker – respectable and soberly dressed in long sleeved shirts to cover the obscene tattoos on his arms and chest; and part-time bikie – gang leader of the 'Devils Disciples' a totally disgusting collection of human waste and scum within the order.

Now with her Daughter Helen dead, beaten, raped and defiled in an inhumane attack, her inner soul glowed white hot with hate. Terry will pay, and pay heavily.

"There's a rather bad wound between your first and second knuckle which looks infected. Also there is some restriction to movement of your knuckle joint, almost as if you have something stuck in there. I really think I must anaesthetize it before I can properly examine you."

"No, just do it without." Terry said with a grin.

The doctor carefully probed the wound. "There is something in there." he said. Taking a pair of forceps, he carefully probed inside the knuckle joint. "Ah, here we are." He dropped the small fragment into a stainless steel bowl on the table to inspect it better. He looked from the white fragment directly into the man's eyes. The man met his stare nonchalantly. The doctor opened his mouth to comment, but looking into the light brown eyes, which were still holding his, he thought better of it. He disinfected the wound, put two small stitches in it and covered it with a surgical dressing. "That should heal quickly." he said. "Just have your GP remove the stitches in a few days time."

"Thanks Doc." With that, he stood, nodded to the doctor, smiled at Mary and walked out.

The doctor stood very still at the table, staring after the man for a while. Mary looked at the fragment in the bowl. It was a human tooth, snapped off at gum level.

* * * * * * * * * * * * *

And so the acid, bitter sweet satisfaction of revenge sweeps over in a flood tide, leaving the grief somewhat more bearable.

But the truth is not what it seems, and the facts are deeply disturbing.

CHAPTER 1

Vanessa and Clyde were twins, until they were 5 or 6 they could not be told apart. They were unusual as far as twins go. Twins of the opposite sex rarely exhibit the same physiological closeness of identical twins. The Machin twins did, their individual sexuality could not be questioned. At 18 they differed greatly in appearance, Clyde was a touch over six foot two, Vanessa was five foot six. He was lean and stringy, she was outstanding!

The Machin family lived on the Silverfield road council estate. Billy Machin, the father of most of the Machin kids, was rough, crude and frequently drunk. All of the kids, along with Enid, and their mother suffered at his hands.

When the twins were 16 years old, Billy arrived home one Sunday afternoon at about 3.25 pm very drunk and belligerent. He stumbled through the kitchen into the lounge "get out of my chair" he growled at Vanessa. As she rose to move out of the chair he staggered across the room and hit her open handed across the face, she fell onto Clyde who was sitting on the arm of the chair. Clyde helped her to her feet; a trickle of blood ran down her top lip from her nose. As Clyde rose his eyes glowed with a ferocity that startled Enid but was lost on Billy who was slumped in the chair watch horse racing. Clyde and Vanessa both had pale green eyes, unlike the rest of the kids whose eyes were brown, a fact which never held any significance to Billy neither did it occur to him that while his IQ was probably

85 the IQ of the twins was nearer to 150. Enid knew, however, their natural father was another Irishman, who for a few short months 16 years earlier had given young and pretty Enid a lot of pleasure at snatched moments in a caravan in which he lived while working on the reservoir. Clyde also inherited another unusual quality which was not to be realized for some time!

The twins both went to the local comprehensive school and were always within a mark of each other in all their exams. Now at 18 they were at a crossroad, they finished high school with top marks and their teacher informed them that their marks qualified them to apply for a place at university. Vanessa wanted to apply Clyde did not. For the first time their paths were set to diverge.

Clyde had taken up karate at the schools night classes and as with everything else he did he excelled. In his environment he was now a loner all his contemporaries and neighbours children had left at 16 to become labourers and apprentices Vanessa was his only confidant at school, at this point they were very close.

On their 18 birthday Clyde and Vanessa, together with a few friends, were dancing in the lounge. Enid was listening to the music as she ironed in the kitchen doorway. At 11.30 pm Billy staggered in, drunk as usual. He looked at the kids laughing and dancing and walked over to Vanessa's new radio on the sideboard picking it up he smashed it on the floor. The room was suddenly silent. " Billy" shouted Enid. Billy turned and hit her across the face with the back of his hand; she raised her hands to her face to ease the smarting of the blow. She did not see Clyde turn or the green glow of his eyes .But she knew this was coming. Billy was a brawler and had many fights both at work as a labourer and the pub; he saw Clyde coming and swung a haymaker. Clyde just bobbed under the blow. Turning he kicked Billy behind his right knee. Billy fell into the sideboard with a crash, breaking bits and pieces of china and photograph frames.

Badly shaken Billy tried to rise. No screamed Enid as Clyde started towards him. The green glow dimmed and Clyde walked out of number 17 and never returned.

Two weeks later Clyde was accepted into the army and Vanessa left for Sheffield University to study medicine.

CHAPTER 2

LIKE EVERYTHING CLYDE HAD DONE, in the army he excelled, within a year he passed out as a junior officer in the Green Howards, a regiment of great tradition. Two years on he applied for and was accepted into the S.A.S, passing out top of his intake. Five years from joining he was the youngest captain in the S.A.S. Twice decorated for bravery during the Fauklands Campaign. He also saw a great deal of action in Northern Ireland.

The S.A.S teaches proficiency in all forms of weaponry and as expected Clyde excelled in them all shooting, archery and explosives. In the service he was a legend in a branch of the armed forces which excelled in all forms of warfare. A visiting marine colonel was so impressed with Clyde he presented him with his own personal hand gun, a customized colt 45 with scrimshawed norwale hand grips, polished slides and adjustable sights .With this weapon Clyde would pile the 75 gram cupro nickel bullets one on top of the other until the bulls eye on the target was a ragged hole 50 mm across.

The twins wrote to each other several times a month. Vanessa, now in her seventh and final year of university, was due to sit her finals to become a doctor three days before her 25th birthday. They made arrangements to meet on their birthday for dinner. Each time they met Clyde marvelled at her beauty and presence. They were sitting in the White Hart having pre-dinner drinks when Clyde excused himself momentarily. Upon his return he noticed several men had joined Vanessa at the table. She stood up to join him. The biggest of the men placed a rough hand on her arm and pulled her down. "Take your hands off her" Clyde said in a low voice. "Piss off" the man said without looking at Clyde. Clyde moved around the table and, almost gracefully, grabbed the man's little finger between his finger and thumb. With a quick twist, it broke with a pop like a snapped carrot. The man screamed and the pub went silent. Still holding the damaged finger, Clyde led the man outside. He released the finger and the man hugged it to his chest. He stared at Clyde. In the sodium lights of the car park, the eyes that looked back at him glowed with a green ferocity. "If I see you again I'll snap your neck like your finger" Clyde said "do you understand". The man nodded sullenly. Vanessa came out to join her brother. They left the man and walked to Clyde's car. After they parted company, Clyde left for Northern Ireland. That night was the last time Clyde saw his sister.

CHAPTER 3

HE HAD ONLY BEEN BACK in Ireland a few days. It was about 1:45am on a Sunday morning when he woke with a start, in the distance a dog barked. It was quite warm but a cold shudder shook him and an indefinable sadness consumed him. He got out of bed and crossed to the basin under the window where he filled a tumbler with water. The glass had only touched his lips when another shudder struck, this one was more violent than the first spilling the water onto his hand, dripping onto the carpet.

Early the next morning Enid phoned Clyde at his barracks in Northern Ireland and told him Vanessa was dead. She had been raped and assaulted, so severe was the assault that the police were reluctant to give Enid any further details. After a shocked silence Clyde said he would come home immediately Clyde applied for compassionate leave and left on the next available air craft.

Clyde flew from Ireland and arrived at the Special SAS barracks in Kent, from there he drove an unmarked company car north headed for Harrogate. He reached his destination just after midday Sunday the 4th.

In the early eighties, in an estate quite close to Harrogate, an Arab of immense wealth and huge importance to the British economy was taken hostage by an Islamic terrorist group. The Prime Minister of the day, although not as blue as his predecessor, immediately ordered the S.A.S. to negotiate with the seemingly uncompromising fundamentalists. The operation, which Clyde was in charge, was extremely successful and resulted in 6 of Islam's chosen martyrs entering the golden gates sooner than they expected.

Before the resulting victory of the SAS, A young Constable named Ron Bateman had been on duty at the estate alone and unarmed, apart from his standard issue truncheon. He observed a black transit van entering the estate and was then suddenly confronted by 6 fanatical, totally psychotic Arabs waving automatic weapons. As he endeavoured to carry out his duty of care, he was gunned down and left for dead. Fortunately for Constable Bateman, the Arabs did not hang around long enough to confirm their target was dead, instead he was left with a severely injured leg. With blood pouring from the wound, he had stemmed the bleeding by tying his tie around his thigh. This is how he was found by Clyde who got him off the estate and to safety in time to save his life.

CHAPTER 4

AFTER ARRIVING HOME AND EXTRACTING all the information he could from his mother, Clyde went straight to the police station.

Chief Inspector Gordon Hollaway was in charge and an incident room had been set up to deal with the attacks. They would only give Clyde very scant details. His sister had been raped, savagely beaten and had died as a result of the injuries.

The details they had so far were sketchy. The night after they'd had dinner together, Clyde had left for Northern Ireland. It was a Saturday and Vanessa was due back at Sheffield Infirmary on Monday where she was residing in the medical students' quarters. She had agreed to meet another student doctor for a night out. At 10.30 they both went into Champagne Charlies, a night club in Harrogate. That was the last time she was seen. The other student doctor gave as much help as possible to the police. She had earlier met some friends inside the night club but had left to go to a party, leaving Vanessa in the company of an Irishman she had met in the there earlier. The man was unknown to any one interviewed. They remembered that he was with two other men about the same age.

In all of the people traced that were there that night, no positive description of the three men could be made. They thought the one talking to Vanessa was Irish, tall and muscular. The doorman/bouncer remembered them arriving, being a bouncer for many years he had dealt with a variety of rough and ugly customers. He recalled that the tall one had troubled him. He had stared at him deliberately from a range of a few feet, the man returned his stare; in the light from the entry, his eyes glittered dangerously. The bouncer was tempted to make a comment to provoke him but for reasons he couldn't explain, decided not to.

As the man walked into the club, the doorman/bouncer noticed his boots, which were unusual. They were made of soft leather and appeared to have no soles; the sides and sole were made of the same leather without a noticeable join. As he pondered these strange boots, a large gang of noisy teenagers entered the doorway and his mind was suddenly occupied. He forgot all about the boots and never thought to mention them to the police.

This was all the information Clyde was given.

As he left the police station Clyde ran into a familiar face. Ron Bateman, now a sergeant, had been expecting to see Clyde considering the circumstances. And even as a policeman used to trauma, when faced with Clyde, he was shocked at his own depth of sympathy for the man. Clyde was not a huge man and from a distance, quite ordinary, but up close he had a certain presence that was impossible not to notice.

"I am so sorry for your loss" said Ron, extending his hand to shake Clyde's. "Thank you," said Clyde "could I perhaps buy you a drink?" "OK" replied Ron "let's pop over the road to Feathers." Here he told Clyde as much as he dared about the investigation.

CHAPTER 5

Aғᴛᴇʀ Cʟʏᴅᴇ ʜᴀᴅ ʟᴇғᴛ ᴛʜᴇ police station he drove to the White Hart Inn where he checked in for the night. He slept fitfully, which wasn't really surprising. At 11:00am he went to Champagne Charlies which was closed. Knowing the premises wasn't unattended he rang the doorbell constantly until eventually it was violently pulled open. It was a very hard looking man facing him from behind the door but his angry face lit up when he recognised Clyde. "Hi Tommy." said Clyde. "Clyde mi boy ho! It's been a long time! Come in, come in." He opened the door wide enough for Clyde to enter and then led him up the stairs. Tommy had been a bouncer for years. He had trained with Clyde at Karate before Clyde had entered the army.

They walked through the empty club and sat on stools at the bar. "Clyde, I'm so sorry about Vanessa." said Tommy as he poured two double shots of Bushmills into two separate glasses and filled them with ice. He handed one to Clyde who asked "Were you here the night it happened." Taking a large swig of his drink, "Yes" he replied. "Tell me Tommy, tell me what you saw." Tommy looked straight at Clyde. "Importantly, tell me about the Irishman." pleaded Clyde. Tommy looked away "I didn't tell the guarda, I'm sorry Clyde" he said regretfully, "but you know how I feel about them." "It's OK Tommy, tell me." Tommy collected his thoughts and turned back to Clyde. "I saw him come in about 9pm. He was a big cocky sod, hard and handy, you know the sort, you've have seen them before. But this one, he was different, sort of aware of himself. I wasn't going to let him in but knew I'd have had a real battle trying to keep him out. When I checked about for him later, he was talking to Vanessa."

Tommy leaned over the bar, "Clyde," he said softly as if he might be overheard "he came in with Crazy Mick. You know him, Clyde?" In a whispered response Clyde said "I know him." With that he stood to leave, his drink untouched. Tommy drank what was left in his glass and then drank Clyde's as well, no point in letting it go to waste. "Good luck boy, oh, good luck.' he said to Clyde's retreating back.

Clyde was half way across the darkened dance floor when Tommy stook up and called after him.

"Wait," he said "I almost forgot he was wearing strange boots. The Irishman, he had these strange boots on."

"What do you mean by strange boots?" asked Clyde. "They were sort of like those Arab boots; you know the ones, the lace up things with no soles?" With that last piece of information Clyde left Champagne Charlies.

CHAPTER 6

CRAZY MICK WAS WELL KNOWN in the area, Clyde had no difficulty in finding which pub he frequented. He had spent the last 2 nights in a row going to Feathers bar in Commercial Street with no sign of Crazy Mick. It was about 8:30pm on the third night when he entered the saloon. He took in his surroundings as he made his way to the bar and then he saw him, Crazy Mick talking to another man with a bandaged hand. Clyde recognised him on sight. As he ordered his drink he watched the men in the mirror and noticed the man with the bandaged hand nod towards him. He was obviously telling Crazy Mick how Clyde had broken his finger.

Crazy Mick was a large coarse featured man; he had long muscular arms covered in ginger hair. Springy hair of the same colour sprouted out of his shirt neck. He stood from the bar and walked over to Clyde closely followed by the man whose finger Clyde had broken in the White Hart. "I want to talk to you" he said aggressively. Outside, they came to a toilet block. "In here" he ordered. The building had concrete walls and floor with a black painted urinal running down one side. "You owe this man 2 months wages for breaking his finger and I am going to collect it, I'll show you how I deal with clever buggers like you."

His method of intimidation was to menace his opponent from close range. He moved in on Clyde to make his presence felt. Most people would have felt fear at this stage but as he moved closer, Clyde moved sideways and kicked down with his heel on Crazy Micks knee. There was a click as his kneecap dislocated under the pressure of the sharp leather heel. He grabbed Clyde by the arm to try and break his fall, as he did this; Clyde caught his arm and used it as a lever. He then placed his foot on his head and forced it into the urinal, pushing his face into the puddles of urine. "Jesus Christ" the muffled curse came from the Irishman, "my fucking leg."

"Tell me about the Irishman with the desert boots!" Clyde ordered. "Jesus Christ" he exclaimed again. Clyde repeated the question as he pushed his head further into the trough. The Irishman groaned heavily before answering "He's The Collector." Clyde released the pressure and allowed him to lift his head somewhat. "What do you mean, The Collector?" Resignedly he answered "He collects the dues for the boys." "Are you talking about the IRA here? Clyde questioned. "Yes," said Crazy Mick "they get 10 pounds for each man on site every month. He comes on the first Saturday each month to collect the money." Clyde needed more, "What is his name?" he demanded. Crazy Mick shrugged. Clyde applied more pressure again to which Crazy Mick responded "Honestly, I don't know. He's only ever called The Collector."

Clyde released Crazy Mick and he sprawled to the floor. Just as he was getting his breath back Clyde bent over and in a low and deliberate tone, loaded with menace, hissed "If you tell anyone what you have told me, especially The boy's I'll rearrange your other knee-cap. Do you understand?" He turned and faced the other man for the first time since they had entered the building, he had not moved through the entire episode, "And that goes for you to." They both nodded sullenly and he left them where they were to contemplate what had just happened.

CHAPTER 7

Longbottom and Crowther Construction were well known to all the local authorities. They tendered on most civil engineering projects, especially reservoirs, as they had a great deal of experience in this field. Mr O'Shaughnessy (known to others as Crazy Mick) was their site foreman and Mr Dalgleath the project manager.

O'Shaughnessy had just finished explaining 'The Organisation's' demands of a 1500 pound amount to be paid monthly for the works. Not having any experience of this before, he told Crazy Mick to ignore the threat. This would prove to be a very unfortunate error. Within a week, 2 Cat D9's were immobilised; one with sugar in the fuel tank, the other mysteriously drew large quantities of sand in through the machine's air intake. The cost of repairs was in the thousands of pounds, the loss of revenue from the machines immobility was over twenty-five thousand pounds.

The Board agreed with Mr Dalgleath that it would be expedient to pay the 1500 pound levy without delay. Arrangements were made for the cash to be hidden in the books as commission. There were no further problems on site. Twelve thousand pounds have been made since the agreement was made.

At first, Crazy Mick had not known who had collected the money. It was always placed in a waterproof package and left in a dustbin with a 'P' marked on the lid in white paint. The bin was placed behind the engineering store on the last Friday of every month. The wages and the package arrived at 10:30am; Crazy Mick placed the package in the dustbin as he left the site at 4:00pm.

Crazy Mick was born in Ballihorrie, on the west coast of Ireland. He went to school in Longha. He was a tough kid and the only time he was ever beaten in a scrap was by a younger, slightly built, shorter boy called Sean. Try as he might, windmilling his long arms, he could not hit the other boy who danced before him like a cat each time he came forward. With lightning speed he stabbed vicious punches into Mick's face, until badly beaten, eyes swollen shut and his wind broken, before kneeing him in the stomach; Crazy Mick fell to the ground grovelling.

Crazy Mick knew enough of The Organisation not to get involved; he kept right out of their way. The negotiations were made, with a hoarse whispering voice, on the site telephone. At 7:30pm on a Friday night, he parked his Datson truck, and entered the shed to collect his flask and empty lunch box that he had left behind when leaving work earlier that day. The sight was dark and empty so he was surprised to hear a metallic clang coming from the direction of the behind the toilet block. The responsibility of pilfering from the site was ultimately his responsibility and he took good care to limit it at all costs. With this in mind, he picked up an axe handle from the corner of the shed, completely forgetting the money in the bin, opened the door and slipped around the side of the shed and down to the back. Peering along the back of the sheds he could see a small saloon car at the side of the toilets with the door open, the interior light giving a dim glow. The bastards are breaking into the store he thought; that's going to cost them.

Silently he inched his way along the back of the line of cabins until he reached the end of the store where he paused trying vainly to see something, anything. He could see nothing but the small car. Without warning, a cold metal tube slid slowly along his neck and came to rest at his ear. He could smell oil, he heard nothing. He could feel the hairs on the back of nick rise and prickle, instinct hold him to stand perfectly still.

A hoarse whisper told him "Do not move. If you move at all, I'll kill you." The voice was familiar. The telephone voice, but more than that, back in his childhood, through pain and suffering, he had heard the same voice say "If you get up now, I'll kill you." Sean McCracken he thought. After the fight at school Michael O'Shaughnessy had attached himself to this sharp articulate lad until he left school. "You wouldn't shoot an old school mate, would you Sean?" Mick asked. For a few seconds, the question hung in the air. Mick heard an intake of breath and knew he was right in the identification of the man standing behind him. "Turn around slowly and drop the pole." said the voice. Mick let go of the pick axe handle and turned slowly. The man stepped back a pace, he was certainly a formidable presence. Taller now than Mick, he had wide shoulders under a black quilted jacket, a lean face, cheek muscles taught. The gun in his hand was a Starr 9mm fitted with a screw on silencer, beads of sweat stood out on Mick's forehead and he felt real fear. For a few second he thought Sean was going to shoot him anyway. He stood silently waiting whatever was coming. Without another word Sean turned on his heel and walked back to the car.

CHAPTER 8

Earlier today had been collection day from Longbottom & Crowther, Friday the 25th. Now Sean stood at the bar drinking Perrier Water. His request for Perrier Water, with ice and lemon, had surprised the barman but Sean's expression had not invited comment. He was a fanatic but a professional. It was early and the pub was not busy. While reflecting on the days events, another customer approached the bar. He was a big heavy man with a dirty bandage on his right hand. Once at the bar, he paused before nervously turning to McCracken.

"Are you the collector?" he asked quietly. Sean turned to look at the man, although greatly surprised by his question he showed no sign. Nervously, again the man spoke "If you are, you would do well to hear me." Sean motioned with his head to a seat at far end of the room. When they were seated he said "Well?" The man swallowed hard. "Well" McCracken said again. "The bastard broke my finger." said the man. Thinking this man may not be the full quid he started to rise from his seat but the man placed a hand on his arm Sean looked at the large red hand and then at the man; he was uneasy, sweat had broken out on his forehead. "The man who broke my finger was asking about your boots, Crazy Mick said he could fix him but Bloody Hell the guy almost killed him" he was babbling. Sean raised a hand, "You had better start at the beginning" he said.

It was 11:30pm when Crazy Mick left Feathers that night. He had been drinking solidly from 8:00pm but years of drinking had given him the ability to hold it well. He walked out and turned left onto New Street, limping badly. He was not a sociable man and had never married. He had moved from site to site for years without any roots holding him back. For the past year, he had lodged at 47 Harlow Terrace with a widow. He had kept the room tidy and not created any problems, 'never crap on your own doorstep" he had often said. He was walking past Walkers Alley when he changed direction, heading instead down the alley. The alley led to the canal where he stood on the tow path and unzipped his trousers, a long stream of urine hit the dark canal water.

Two dull plops, even in the quiet of the evening, went unnoticed by anyone. Crazy Mick hit the water face down and floated across to the other side. Back on New Street, a small saloon car pulled away from the parking area opposite the Post Office and moved out into the light traffic. It was an ordinary little car attracting no attention.

Clyde sat on the bed in his room at the White Hart. He now had someone to focus on – The Collector. But he would now be long gone from the district back to Ireland.

Next day, Clyde checked out and drove to SAS Headquarters where he requested semi-permanent leave and caught the next military plane to Belfast.

CHAPTER 9

Shirley Wilson was 17 years old, weighed 18 stone and had Downs Syndrome. When she was born it was apparent seconds after the birth that something was wrong. The nurse had taken the baby directly out of the delivery room as soon as she had been delivered. Polly Wilson had suffered through the labour with Shirley; she had been breach and had weighed 10½ pounds.

Jack Wilson had been present at the birth; not his wishes, Polly had insisted he be there. He hadn't found it a pleasant experience. Strangely though, he had developed an unbelievable love and warmth for the strange lumpy baby that cried and cried and cried.

Polly was ashamed of the baby and it was Jack who brought her up and played with her, spending all his spare time trying to amuse the little girl. At the age of 6 she was accepted into a council sponsored home for mentally handicapped children. Jack would fetch her and bring her home every night.

CHAPTER 10

Jack Wilson was a chemist, owning 2 very successful shops. One was in the town centre and the other about 3 miles out in the suburbs. He was a very methodical man and took a great deal of pride in his attention to detail.

The whole of Jack's life had revolved around Shirley; he did not see her as the rest did, only as his little girl. At first he could not accept that his little girl had been so viciously assaulted. For a long time he walked about as if in a dream. It was about three weeks before his methodical mind began to slowly overcome the numbing grief only to be replaced by the smouldering hatred for the person who carried out the attack. It began to burn into a white hot fire.

The police, it would appear, were getting nowhere. Jack began to brood about the man that had done this; tried to imagine what sort of an animal would do such a thing. He decided that he would seek retribution himself. He would find the person and destroy him, just as he had done to a defenseless child. He opened a file on the man and began to fill it.

Firstly he decided that this person, whoever they may be, had to be a man because he could not believe this could be carried out by a woman. Going on from this assumption it may be the most serious offence, but perhaps not the only one.

Jack had very competent Assistance Chemists now employed in each of his shops; this allowed him plenty of spare time. He started by going to the library to read back editions of the local newspaper.

Slowly and remorselessly he read each edition, making notes of anything he thought may be of use to him. Two items came to light. The first was about 2 years ago. In a wooded area, known as Rooks Copse, a dog was found with its stomach slit from it genitals to its breast bone. The wretched dog was still alive when it was found and had to be destroyed. There were no further details, just a report of the facts.

The second item of interest was more recent. Behind some garages on the Silverfield Road Council Estate, adjacent to Rooks Copse, a tramp had been sleeping. Hearing screams, people living adjacent to the garages rushed out of their houses in time to save the tramp, he was on fire. At first it was reported that he had probably fallen asleep with a lit cigarette and it had set fire to his bundle of rags and papers. However, a subsequent report stated that the fire was caused by petrol. The tramp was reported as saying that someone had just poured petrol over him and then set him on fire.

The two seemingly unrelated events occurred with a few hundred yards of the Silverfield Road Council Estate.

CHAPTER 11

After Shirley, was born his wife changed. Polly could no longer enjoy sexual relationships at all, not that she was overly sexual before, but since the birth there was nothing. Jack had started frequenting a local massage parlor called Eve's. Here in darkened surroundings, smelling of baby powder and Johnson's baby oil, he relaxed. Behind the locked cubicle doors the girls performed whatever was requested from them, for a price. Jack always had Belinda (who's real name was Anne Baxter). He had, over the years, built up a friendly relationship with her; and she in turn treated him as a valued customer. She would carry out things for him she did not offer to other more casual customers.

After one of his weekly rituals, of massage with oil and a combination of sexual gratifications, they sat together on the massage bed; Jack with a large white bathrobe around his waist, she naked, her body still streaked with oil. Jack look at her, "Thanks." he said and she smiled back at him. "You must get some really weird types in here don't you?" asked Jack casually.

"Oh yes." she said "I tell you Johnnie (that is what she knew Jack as), you wouldn't believe it. Some of the pranks they get up to. There's a high court judge comes in, he wears frilly undies and he insists on mopping the floor while the girls hit him with canes. What a scream!!"

"Do you get any violent weirdo's?" asked Jack.

"No, not usually." she said. "Only one in all the time I've been here"

"Oh, what happened." he pushed, trying not to show too much interest.

"Well one time this bloke came in, he took Amanda, you know the black girl?" Jack nodded. "Well he took her and then apparently wanted to do it with a big rubber dildo."

"A what?' interjected Jack.

"You know; a big fake prick." she said. "Anyway, when Amanda refused he got really violent, slashed her across the tits with a Stanley knife."

"Good God." said Jack.

"Good God alright, we were terrified. Amanda was screaming her head off."

"What happened next?" asked Jack.

"Well," she continued "Harry, he runs the taxi business downstairs, heard the commotion and came running up. He's quite a big bastard and the bloke calmed down when he saw him come in. Harry got the bloke out of there without too much more to do. Harry gets a freebie now and then for his effort."

"What did the police say then?" said Jack.

"We never called the police. It's best to keep a low profile where they are concerned. Amanda got stitched up good as new, at some Asian doctor in town, no questions asked." smiled Belinda.

"What was he like, this bloke?"

"I never really saw him," said Belinda "just a glimpse as Harry bustled him out; young 22 or 23 maybe, fair scruffy hair, tall." She bent to pick up her clothes, "Would you like a sauna?"

"No, thanks," said Jack "I must be going."

Jack knew who Harry was as he was a regular at the chemist. When he left the massage parlor, he went straight into White Ace Taxis. "Hi," he said to Harry, "how's business?"

"Oh not too bad, Jack. Been upstairs then?" he said with a grin.

Jack smiled in return "Yes, I've just delivered them penicillin; they have all got a dose."

"Bloody Hell!" exclaimed Harry, "Don't even joke about things like that." Jack laughed. "Seriously though Jack, I was very sorry to hear about Shirley, that is a dreadful business."

"Thanks." Jack mustered, becoming serious again. "I wanted to ask you something Harry, the bloke who caused a rumpus upstairs, do you remember him?"

"No," said Harry, "I'd never seen him before or since."

"Can you describe him to me, anything you can remember?"

Harry stared at Jack and was about to say something else but changed his mind, then said "Young, about 25, slim build with unruly blond hair. He had the word 'Bernard' tattooed on one of his hands. He was on something, I'm sure." said Harry.

"On something, what do you mean?" asked Jack.

"You know; drugs." said Harry. "His eyes were funny; the pupils were like pin heads." "What are you up to?" he asked Jack.

"An eye for an eye." said Jack.

"What do you think, this bloke did that to………"

"Harry," said Jack firmly and sharply, "forget it, please."

"OK Jack, mum's the word eh."

CHAPTER 12

ON THE SILVERFIELD ROAD COUNCIL Estate was a fish and chip shop run by Fred Brownlow. Jack started to frequent this shop on several occasions chatting to Fred, and twice buying fish and chips which he dropped into a waste bin on his way home. On or about the fourth time in the shop he found it to be empty of any other customers, he placed his order. When it was done, he opened the packet and leant on the counter to eat them. Fred was frying fish, first dipping haddock into the batter then placing it into the hot fat.

"Do you get a lot of trouble around here?" asked Jack making small talk.

"No," said Fred, "a few drunks at around 11pm when the pubs close but no real trouble."

"I bet you have trouble with that Bernard, don't you?" quizzed Jack.

"Bernard McIvor? Not anymore, least not for 3 years anyway." he said and laughed.

"They should have given the bastard life if you ask me." he continued.

Bingo thought Jack. "Oh, they have caught him then?"

Just then a girl came out from the back of the shop with a bucket of chips. She lifted the lid on the next pan and tossed the chips into the fat. The fat hissed and spat as she quickly closed the lid on the pan. "Yes," she answered for Fred, 'he got three years just last week. Did you know him?" she asked.

"He used to go out with one of the girls who worked for me." said Jack.

"Well, she's better off without that one." she said.

"What did he do that finally got him caught?" asked Jack

"Slashed a bouncers face at a night club."

Jack looked up the electoral roll for the McIvor's in Silverfield Road and found the house number – 126. The next night he called around. His knock was answered by a woman in her late fifties. Her tired face was heavily made up and she was wearing a full length petticoat. "Yes" she said aggressively.

"My name is Johnson," Jack said smiling pleasantly, only to be interrupted by the woman saying "Well, what do you want?"

"Can I speak with Bernard?" he asked.

The woman laughed, "Not unless you've got a bloody loud voice." Jake appeared puzzled. "He's inside," she said, "in Jail."

"Good Lord." exclaimed Jack. "I'm sorry."

"I'm not." said the woman. "I hope they keep the bastard forever."

"It's just that I have some of his possessions." Jack continued.

"They're probably nicked anyway." said the woman.

"Nevertheless, I would like to return them if I could. Where.... um....where?" said Jack lamely.

"Wakefield Prison." said the woman. "Here, give them to me and I'll give them to the social worker to take to him." she said, laughing again.

Jack handed her the plastic bag.

Jack had placed several odd items in the bad that he had bought at the Oxfam shop in town. An old Beattles Penny Lane LP, a pair of faded jeans and a grey pullover. He considered the 5 pound he had spent to be a good investment. Strange though, he thought, that the woman hadn't asked how he had come across Bernard's things. He had worked out a reply should she have asked, but it was obviously of little interest to her.

The next day, Jack purchased a pad of notepaper from a stationer in town together with matching envelopes. He then bought a bottle of cheap perfume. With these supplies he sat to down and wrote.

Dear Bernard,

You do not know me as yet, but you will. I yearn for the day that you are released. I have always loved you but have until now been unable to tell you. Every night when I go to bed I take the thought of having your naked body next to mine. Oh, how I would love to make love to you over and over again. I would let you do anything you wanted to me. I love you so much. My passion for you grows with every minute. I just had to contact you at last.

Your ever loving,
Belinda xxxxxxx

Jack poured a little of the scent into the envelope, sealed it and addressed it to:

Mr. Bernard McIvor
HM Prison
Highthope Road
Wakefield

When he was done he posted the letter. He waited a week then posted another. The second letter was in similar vain to the first only it had a little more sexual undertones.

Above the chemist shop in town Jack had a flat. It had remained empty since he had evicted the last tenants, No. 3 Vallow Lane, with its own entrance from a side street, would serve him well.

On the third letter he sent he placed a return address at the top, 3 Vallow Lane. Anxiously he checked the post to the flat every day. It was on the fourth day that a letter arrived with *HM Prison, Wakefield* printed on the back.

CHAPTER 13

BERNARD INHALED THE CHEAP PERFUME from the letters laid out on his chest. He lay on the bed in his cell. Charlie Pinks, lay on the bunk below him, snoring thinly. Bernard spat on his hand. After satisfying himself, he wiped his hand and wilting member on Charlie's towel then threw it back over the chair at the end of the bed with a giggle. Stupid old Pratt, the only time I can have a good wank is when he's asleep he thought.

For the 20th time, he read the last letter and pondered on the contents. It worried him greatly, 'How could she know about the dog and tramp', no-one knew, he had told no-one and he was sure nobody had been around to witness the incidents.

At 7:30am a metallic clang signaled that the door system had opened automatically. Bernard picked up his towel soap and razor and stood beside the door. Charlie, seeing the stains of dried semen on his towel, started to protest, "You dirty bastard." he shouted. "You've wanked on my towel again. I'm going to report you this time."

"Shut up you bloody old fool." hissed Bernard as the door swung open.

On the metal decking outside, spaced about 4 cells apart, stood 5 warders. The nearest stood about 10 feet to the left, just too far to be able to see completely into the cell. Charlie was creating sufficient noise to attract the warder's attention. Using his towel like a whip, Bernard flicked the end into Charlie's face. The end cracked like a whip into his eye blinding him. He yelped and dropped his things putting his hands up to his face.

The warder appeared at the door. "What's going on here?" he enquired.

"No problem." said Bernard "I must have caught him with my towel as I picked it up." he added glibly.

The warder went over to Charlie, "Are you alright old timer?"

In his present state Charlie decided on a different course of action than Bernard had expected. "No problem officer." was his reply.

Charlie worked in the kitchen. He had worked there for the last 3 years. As a habitual criminal, his last sentence had been 7 years for complicity in an armed robbery. He was to receive 1,500 pound as a lookout. Unfortunately for him, he was picked up at the scene along with the getaway driver and another extremely dangerous character by the name of Frank Rylie.

The rest of the gang got away with nearly ¾ of a million in used bank notes. Despite concerted effort by the police, Charlie had remained silent throughout his time in police custody and indeed throughout the trial. He had received no money yet. However, he was informed by Frank Rylie that 25,000 pound had been deposited in his name in a Building Society in Bradford. Already the money had earned another 5,000 pound in interest.

Charlie had spent most of his adult life in jails. He was not a violent man, in fact he was quite frail and delicate looking, but he knew the rules and dodges of jail life. Working in the kitchen had several advantages. It was easy work and a lot of favours could be earned from kitchen supplies. Charlie had had enough of Bernard's petty cruelty; having taken one too many liberties with his shy and retiring nature.

Frank Rylie's ugly features contorted and his yellow teeth clamped tight together as the strain forced back his lips. On either side of his short bull neck, cords of muscle bunched. He laid on the bench, across his chest, the weight bar with 175lbs on each end; suck, suck blow, his breath escaped in sharp whistles. Push! The bar rose. Harold Smith stood at his head to help if he couldn't make it. "Push Frank, push." he cried in encouragement. Slowly the hairy arms straightened, almost there, the arms began to tremble with the tremendous strain. The tremble spread to his pectorals. "Push Frank." Harold cried again. Another 2 inches and the arms locked; the movement complete. Harold caught the bar and lifted it onto the supports. "Christ Frank, 20lbs up on last week."

Dark sweat stains showed in the centre of his tee-shirt, he sat up and grinned. Charlie waited until Frank's breathing had settled. "Now then Charlie, have you come to work out?" asked Frank.

Charlie looked around the gym, "Too late now Frank." he said with a smile.

"What's wrong with your eye?" Frank said, seeing Charlie's red and bloodshot eye.

"Spot of bother with my cell mate. That's what I've come here to see you about." he replied.

"Come on old timer," Frank said, rising up from the bench, "I'm through now, let's hit the shower."

Charlie sat on the wooden slatted bench. Frank stood under the hot shower, he looked deformed. For three years now he had spent all his spare time and energy body building, now great slabs of muscle covered his hairy shoulders and chest. His biceps were so enlarged it was difficult to bend his arms. Huge thigh and calf muscles were all out of proportion to his tiny waist. He soaped his abundant genitalia.

"So Charlie, who are you in with?" Frank asked.

"A bloke called Bernard." replied Charlie.

"Do you know him Harold." he asked his companion.

"Yes, tall bloke in for 3 years." replied Harold.

Frank grinned through the soap, "What do you want Charlie, just the frighteners?" "That will do nicely Frank, thanks." People spent time in hospital recovering from Frank's frighteners, Charlie reflected. As he got up to leave, he left a white parcel in full view on the bench.

"This one's free Charlie." said Frank. "Yeah thanks Frank, so is the parcel."

Later, in his cell, Frank opened the parcel. His eyes widened when he saw the contents. "Bloody hell Charlie!" he muttered, "You could have had the lid slammed down on the bloke for this." The parcel contained 250 cigarettes and an oz of Lebanese Gold.

Bernard was relaxing in the chair with his eyes closed, he thought about Belinda. Suddenly he was aware of movement; the 5 or 6 other prisoners who had been in the room were leaving. Bernard turned, standing inside the room at the left of the door, was a prisoner with his arms folded, leaning with his back to the wall. As the last of the inmates left the recreation room another man that Bernard had not seen before entered. The first man closed the door and stood as he had earlier, arms folded and back to the door. The second man grinned menacingly. Not comprehending, Bernard thought idly how strange the man looked. Bernard was nearly six foot, but this man was not more that five feet tall and as he shambled across the room, looked more like an ape; tufts of hair spouted out of his tee-shirt. The sleeves were cut away to reveal huge arms, covered with black hair. He stopped in front of Bernard and looked up at him.

"Bernard my dear, you have won first prize." he said, still smiling.

"What are you talking about?" asked Bernard uneasily.

The grin faded from Frank's face. "Charlie & I have been talking and he was asked me to ask you nicely to stop wanking on his towel."

Bernard tried to step backwards to move out of the man's closeness, as he did Frank raised his arm and jerked forward grabbing a handful of Bernard's trousers, including the whole of his wedding tackle. Bernard gasped, the grip tightened, the muscles in the arm bunched and jerked, the lips drew back from the yellow teeth in a grin.

The power of the man's grip was awesome. Bernard could feel himself fainting as the relentless power seemed to increase. He tried to scream but the sickening grip on his testicles prevented him from even opening his mouth. At the edge of unconsciousness, his eyes closed, his head swimming, the man released his grip and Bernard sank to the floor. He felt himself being lifted up. He could hardly believe it; the man had hold of his ankle and his bicep and lifted him like a rag doll, placing him in the chair. Through the mists of pain he heard a hoarse whisper in his ear, "If you give Charlie any more problems, I'll rip your balls out completely!" With that the two men left. As the blood flowed back into his crushed testicles, he felt the first tingle of pins and needles.

After a few minutes Bernard had recovered sufficiently to stand, holding onto the furniture, he managed to get to the door. Dizzy and unsteady on his feet, he stood holding weakly onto the back of a chair. For the first time in his 24 year existence he felt real fear. Waves of nausea swept up from the pit of his stomach. Like an ink stain, a black blotch appeared at the edge of his consciousness which spread across the back of his eyes. Slowly his brain blacked out and he crumpled up on the recreation room floor.

Bernard came too, slowly, to find himself in the prison hospital. A metal cage over his middle kept the bedclothes away from him, he felt queasy. A white coated doctor walked over to the bed, "Ah, McIvor," he said. "How do you feel?"

"Christ!" he said "Where am I?"

"In the prison hospital," the doctor answered.

A shudder went through Bernard's body as he remembered Frank's grin. "What am I doing here?" he asked.

"You collapsed in the recreation room, something of a mystery really" he said with a grim face. "I'm afraid we have some rather bad new for you."

"What do you mean bad news?" Bernard asked, "How long have I been in here?"

"Since yesterday," the doctor replied "Now please don't get alarmed," he went on "but unfortunately the surgeon has had to remove one of your testicles and the remaining one is badly damaged and may also have to be removed." He gave him a moment to take in the news. "The governor is waiting to speak to you. Do you feel up to it?" Bernard didn't answer. No balls! Oh my God! he thought no balls! That wasn't the end of it though, the next day the surgeon had to remove the right testicle also. The surgeon, a cynical man, said to the shocked nurse "I hope he's not married, because he'll never again get a hard on."

For the first two weeks he just lay in bed. He would speak to nobody. The implications of what had happened physically were carefully explained to him but no-one could tell me what would subsequently happen to his mental state. Bernard was not very intelligent and had a nasty violent nature, with a high tendency to sexual perversion. Like most sexual deviants, he was carful to hide it from view.

Having a low IQ, he had never looked inside himself for answers; he took life as it came and never let an opportunity pass to indulge his unpleasant nature. The removal of his testicles caused several personality changes. Not as he imagined, like growing breasts or lightening of his voice; instead it drove his violent sexual nature deeper into his subconscious, now there was no release by masturbation.

Charlie Pinks lay on his bunk with his hands behind his head; he had the cell to himself. Word had filtered out what had happened to Bernard. He was glad he had asked Frank to help rather than complaining to the warder. He was surprised however, that Frank had caused so much damage with the 'frightening'. With good behaviour he would be out in 18 months time. This time, he thought, I'll retire. Over 30,000 pound waited for him in the Building Society.

CHAPTER 14

In St Mary's Street, Belfast there is a bar called O'Grady's. Clyde was sitting in a corner seat near the window. A seedy looking man in a shabby brown sports coat, which looked a size and a half too large for him, came through the door walking uneasily up to the bar. "A Bushmills and water." he said in a whisper. The barman placed a tumbler on the counter with a measure of gin in it. From a "Black and White" whisky mug on the bar the man poured a splash of water into the glass. The bar was almost empty; another man sat on a stool reading 'The Dublin Echo' and a young couple were huddled over a table engrossed in each other. The seedy man glanced around the bar; he gave no sign of recognising Clyde.

Clyde stood and walked through, past the bar, to the door at the rear of the bar. Across the passage were the toilets. He entered and pushed open each of the two cubicles to check for occupancy. Satisfied they were empty, he stood patiently waiting. A few minutes later the seedy man came in. He looked pinched and uneasy.

"Jesus Christ Boyo, you've picked a ripe one this time," he said to Clyde "don't involve me with this one." he continued with real fear in his voice. "The Collector for the main land is Sean McCracken; he is the most dangerous man ever to come across the border. He is the Chief Logistics Officer for the splinter group known as 'The Sons of Erin'. In fact, he founded the group with another lively bastard known as 'Quiet O'Rourke'. He's been known as this since his vocal chords were cut by the Ulster men."

"I know Quiet O'Rourke, he's on record having been caught and served time for robbery, but the other one is not recorded." said Clyde.

"He is as dangerous as anyone I've ever met." said the man. "Why do you want information privately on him?"

Clyde didn't answer. He held out a 20 Irish Note. The man took it and turned to go. Stopping in the passage, he turned to Clyde "I've never dealt with a straighter man than you and I admire you greatly. The man you seek is as evil as the Devil himself. I should say as good at killing as you are. You will need a great deal of luck and surprise to 'hole in one' this one." With that, he turned down the passage into the side street, his shoulders hunched against the rain, and he was gone.

Clyde returned to his seat and stared out the window, it was raining hard. Looking down the road he saw them coming towards the front door, a gang of youths, one of whom he recognised as Jimmy Gregory from the Gym at the army camp. He worked on the base as a civilian in the radiography unit. His father was a prominent man in Northern Irelands' political circle. The lads cam into the bar and filled the room with their noisy banter.

At first, he went unnoticed while the lads were busy ordering their drinks and then Jimmy turned and caught sight of Clyde. "Hey! What are you doing here?" he shouted over the noise, clearly pleased to see him. "Come over here and meet my friends." Clyde picked up his glass and walked over to the noisy group.

"Have a drink Clyde." said Jimmy. "OK, I'll have a half." Clyde replied. He was introduced to the 'gang' and spent some time exchanging banter with them all.

Sometime later, while the lads were arguing over a pool game in the other room, Clyde and Jimmy were alone. "I was hoping for a quiet word with you Jimmy, I want you to check someone out with your father for me." "Sure." Jimmy replied without hesitation, he had done things like this for Clyde before.

"See what you can find out on Sean McCracken." asked Clyde.

"No problem Clyde, who is he?" asked Jimmy, intrigued.

"I believe he is one of the leaders of the 'Sons of Erin' but that's all I can tell you for now.

He accepted this from Clyde "OK," he said "I'll talk to Dad and meet you at the gym tomorrow lunchtime and let you know how I went." With that they said goodnight and Jimmy returned to his mates.

The next day, Clyde had just completed his fourth set of abdominals on the inclined board when the door burst open and Jimmy came through carrying his sports bag. "I'll be with you in a second." he called to Clyde as he made his way to the changing room, returning a short time later in shorts, vest and training shoes.

He jumped onto the exercise bike to warm up, "Dad would like you to come over tonight." he said.

"Well, what did he have to say about 'our man' Jimmy?" asked Clyde.

"That's what he wants to see you about. Apparently there are very few people who even know your man's name, even less that believe he exists at all."

"What do you mean?" asked Clyde sitting up from the bench.

"You'll have to discuss that with Dad tonight, how about 7pm?" he said.

"I'll see you then." replied Clyde and left the gym.

Clyde walked up the driveway; this was the fist time he had been to the Gregory's house, although Jimmy had invited him many times. The house was on Manse Lane, an expensive leafy suburb on the outskirts of Belfast. Patrick Gregory was left a small builder's company by his father, now it was the largest earthmoving contractor in Northern Ireland. The large stone built house stood on five acres with well-kept gardens. A wall surrounded the gardens, shielding the house from the road. At the top of the driveway stood ten-foot gates; an aluminium panel with a grille and intercom button set in the wall beside. Clyde pressed the button.

"Yes." came a voice from the grille.

"Clyde Machin to see Me Gregory."

"Just a moment." said the voice. After a few seconds, the gates slowly opened. Clyde proceeded up to the house. Taking in his surroundings he noticed several surveillance cameras on his way to the front door and he could see dogs at the back. The dogs were not barking, guard dogs like those don't bark, silent killers, Rottweilers. He could hear them whining softly, he could imagine them trying to force their heavy jawed heads through the chain-link fence of their pens.

As he approached the front door it was opened by a large, florid faced man with pleasant, powerful smile. "Welcome Mr Machin" he boomed as he firmly shook his visitors hand. Clyde could see why he was successful; he liked him instantly, as he had his son.

After the greetings, they headed to the study. "It is pleasure to meet you Mr Machin, Jimmy talks of nothing else but yourself. Will you have a glass?" he asked.

"Thanks." said Clyde accepting the cut crystal glass.

"Please sit down." he indicated a large leather chair, one of two in front of a log fire. As Clyde sat, Patrick Gregory sank into the other chair, holding his glass out at arms length; he stared through the amber liquid at the flames of the fire. "Tell me Mr Machin, why do you want to know about 'The Wolf'."

"Who?" asked Clyde.

"'The Wolf', that is the name that Sean McCracken is known by within the Organisation." he turned to face Clyde, "I get the feeling that his request is personal." Clyde hesitated, and he continued "If I am to trust you, you must tell me the truth!"

"I believe he raped and killed my sister," he said in a voice barely more than a whisper "and if that is so, I intend to execute him."

CHAPTER 15

Patrick sat on the hard wooden chair. He liked Clyde a great deal and knew instinctively that he could be trusted. But who would be using whom! That worried him greatly. He had always been fair in his dealings with his fellow man and it had repaid him handsomely. Now he had to be careful how he orchestrated the next move. There were big stakes at risk.

"The lodge is properly tiled." he heard the Inner Guard state.

"The next care?" said the Worshipful Master.

"To see that none but masons are present!" said the Senior Warden.

Patrick rose from his seat in the East. "I would like to have a chat when you can spare me a moment Donal." he said to his chief constable.

"Right you are Patrick, urgent is it?"

"Yes," Patrick replied "Very".

"OK," said Donal "Can it wait until we have finished the toasts?" They both laughed.

The two men had grown up together. Donal's father had worked for Patrick's father and the two lads had gone to school together, so their friendship had deep roots; both protestant and fiercely opposed the Nationalists and their terror tactics. Patrick took two glasses and a bottle of Chivas Regal back to the table.

"Off the record Patrick?" asked Donal.

"Off the record." confirmed Patrick.

"Right you are then Patrick, fire away!"

Patrick poured out two measure of whiskey and handed a glass to Donal. Patrick took a large swig of his own drink "Operation Dust Bowl." he said.

Donal's expression never altered "Go on." he said

"How successful has it been?" Donal looked hard at Patrick.

"My God," he said at last "You never fail to surprise me Paddy, just how much do you know?"

"Operation Dust Bowl," said Patrick. "an all out attempt to dry up the flow of money to the Organisation."

"Yes, undercover and highly secret. How the devil did you learn about it?" said Donal. "Oh, don't answer that, you wouldn't tell me anyway. I hope you know where your loyalties lay Paddy. What's the urgency anyway?"

"You must forgive me if I speak in a roundabout way," said Patrick "but I only have the good of Ireland at heart, you do believe that, don't you Donal?" He nodded his agreement.

"As you know, or suspect, I have to pay just like every builder and contractor in Ireland, and a lot of the Mainland. If I came to you, you couldn't protect every single one of my machines spread out over the country. And if I refused, do you know what damage a half a pound of sugar will do in a fuel tank?" Donal just nodded, he knew that Patrick was saying was true and known by every building contractor and plant hire firm in the country. "We have to pay to stay in business. I hate it, it goes against everything I believe in." said Patrick. His face suffused with blood and his veins stood out on his neck. He paused to recover and allow his blood pressure to sink back to normal. Donal looked at him and smiled "It's no bloody laughing matter." said Patrick angrily.

"I'm sorry," said Donal "I didn't intend to make light of the problem. It's just that you look like one of Granny O'Grady's Turkey Cocks, all red and indignant." They stared at each other for a few minutes, and then burst into peals of laughter. "Do you remember that Christmas and those bloody turkeys? I couldn't sit down comfortably until New Year." said Donal. The laughter subsided and they were quiet for a few minutes. "Donal," said Patrick "it's not working, is it?"

Donal looked sympathetically at Patrick "You answered your own question," he said "you still paying."

Patrick poured out another two stiff tots from the Chivas bottle and asked "What if the collectors were to become, let's say, subjected to a little free-lance terror?" Donal leaned forward, suddenly very interested. Patrick continued "Well, there are only three and they have to be a bit special."

"Yes." said Donal "they must be clean, without record, unknown almost, to be able to slip backward and forward over the border and across the water."

"The collector's are the best men the Organisation have." said Donal. "You are right, they have to be anonymous."

"I know the identity of one of them." said Patrick. "He collects on the mainland. I don't know the bastard that collects from me though!"

Donal shook his head "I don't suppose you are willing to share that information with me Patrick?'

"Oh yes," said Patrick "but I have a much better proposition for you than just sharing information."

CHAPTER 16

Asmall white pickup, with GREGORY's painted on each door, pulled onto the site. Picking up his white hard hat from the passenger seat along with his notebook and tape Clyde got out of the car. Patrick Gregory's blue 560 Mercedes pulled in behind the small pickup. Patrick whistled loudly and waved his arms at a man in a dark blue donkey jacket standing near a large machine digging a deep hole on the site.

"Over here Graham." he shouted. As the man approached he was introduced to another man he hadn't seen before. "This is Clyde; he is carrying out a survey on our machinery for insurance purposes. Clyde this is Graham, the site foreman."

After two days of introductions like the first, Clyde began to realise just how large and extensive was Patrick Gregory's business; twenty-five sites, including three in Southern Ireland. Carrying out this fictitious job would enable him access to all the sites at any time.

Patrick had done a deal with Donal. That night after lodge, without revealing Clyde's identity, he had gotten a free hand for him. Access to police information (through Patrick) direct to Donal and a clamp down on police for follow up on any action taken by Clyde. For his part, Patrick had given a guarantee to dry up the flow of funds from the construction industry by stopping at least one of the collectors collecting.

Jimmy worshipped Clyde. He knew that Clyde was carrying out some sort of undercover job and he pestered him to be included, sensing adventure. Clyde however, liked Jimmy tremendously and was determined to keep away from anything remotely dangerous.

The instructions for delivery were changed every month by a telephone call to Gregory's head office in Belfast. As the first payment due after Clyde had started was to be collected in Southern Ireland, they agreed to wait until the next delivery hoping for a more convenient location. When the call came, they were advised the delivery would be at the new hospital site in North Garde Road. The preparations began.

At 4:00pm $2,750 was placed in a cement bag and left under the seat of a JCB, registration number 35YTAB, parked under the newly erected steelwork of the North Wing of the new hospital as instructed. At 5:30pm Clyde parked his white pickup in the southern entrance. Under the steel framing the dark structure showed up against the night sky, the concrete formwork giving the steel skeleton some substance on each floor. Clyde took out a gun and duffle bag from under the seat and slung them over his shoulder. Quickly he went up the bare concrete steps to the first floor and across the steel pans to the South Wing. In front of him the sodium lights of the main road cast a yellow glare into the darkened hospital car park. The steel pans on the floor above kept the 1st floor relatively dark. A wooden cabin had been hoisted up for the foreman; Clyde opened the door and went inside. He placed the gun cover on the bench and untied the leather straps. He slid out the dark grey armalite rifle from the duffle bag and night sight. Using the specially prepared brackets he fitted the sight to the rifle. The glass in the cabin window had not yet been fitted. He stood back in the darkness, and using sight, swept across the car park. In the green eerie glow of the eye piece, he read the JCB's registration number 35YTAB. Happy with the arrangements he sat on the bench and poured a coup of coffee from the flask he had placed in the duffle bag. He took the cup and stood so he could see out the glassless window, careful not to expose himself to view.

He was not sure how long he had been standing there when suddenly a small flame flared up at the far end of the site then died away just as quickly. Someone had lit a cigarette. At the far end of the site several vehicles were parked, two of Gregory's transit vans and one from the formwork contractors, a small mobile crane and a dark blue unmarked transit. Through the scope, he could see at least three men in the last vehicle. The man who had lit a cigarette took a drag on it, in the scope it flamed a greenish red.

Jimmy held his breath; he had been there a whole 10 minutes before he had noticed the other man. Now he had no idea whether he had been spotted. Against the street lighting the man was quite noticeable but, Jimmy thought, looking back into the building it was not easy to see. Without moving his head he looked into the interior. He could not see easily, but perhaps he had not been spotted. Then he heard a car door open, a small noise in the silence of the night.

In the green light Clyde watched the young man with the curly hair and earring open the truck door, the door had dropped and scraped on the sill before it swung freely. The man got out of the car and walked casually over to the JCB and picked up the cement bag from under the seat. As he placed his hand on the van door to close it Clyde squeezed the trigger. The 7.35mm bullet passed through his hand (smashing three main bones) and into the door handle. The man dropped the bag and staggered backward clutching his hand to his chest in shock. An engine started and the car door he had left moments ago flew open "Get in quickly!" a voice shouted. The man staggered toward the van as it started forward and half fell into the open door. With a roar, the van shot across the site, tyres spinning, the door flapping against the side, out of the entrance and down the road.

Jimmy had heard the shot and seen the orange muzzle flash come from the small shed. The other man raised his hand, Jimmy could see he had a hand gun with a fat black tube on the end that make it look unwieldy, he know it was a silencer. Up to that point Jimmy had convinced himself the man was unaware of his presence. He was wrong! He turned slightly towards Jimmy, and before he knew what was happening Jimmy saw the orange eye and heard a dull plop. Jimmy received a blow below his left shoulder that knocked him to the ground, then nothing.

Clyde had heard the plop and instinctively dropped to the floor. Seconds later he heard two more plops followed by two sharp splinters as two bullets ripped through the light timber wall at chest height. Clyde wriggled to the door, the heavy customised colt in his right hand. The door was badly fitted, leaving a gap of an inch between the floor and the bottom of the door, allowing Clyde to peer out. Nothing! He could see nothing and hear nothing, everything was quiet. Feeling very vulnerable, he came to his knees and gently pushed open the door, carefully and quietly. Assessing his surroundings, he sprang from the shed, leapt about 2 yards, and laid flat on the steel pans. He still could see nothing. Puzzled, Clyde thought desperately, where did the first shot go? What or who had staked him out? Having no answers, he walked carefully across the floor to in the direction of where the gunman must have stood, judging from the position of the bullets. At the stairwell he paused and turned, the gunman must have stood right here he thought. From here there was a clear view of the TCB and into the hut. Clyde was angry with himself, he had been lax, convinced that he was anonymous, he had placed himself in a vulnerable position. He would have to be much more careful in future. The Man, The Organisation had put one over on him.

A slight noise, over to his left in the darkness, instantly put him back on the alert. He went down into a crouch. Straining his eyes, he stared into the darkness. Stealthily, and on high alert, he ran at a half crouch in the direction the noise had come from. It was there, sprawled over the bracing, that he found Jimmy. He now realised where the first bullet had landed. Desperately, he felt for the pulse in Jimmy's neck. It was with a flood of relief that he felt the steady beat. Carefully, afraid of what he would find, he examined Jimmy. The left side of his tracksuit was soggy, and he found that the bullet had entered his chest just below his collar bone and exited just under the shoulder blade. His breathing was regular but it was obvious that he had lost a lot of blood.

It took the ambulance team just 35 minutes to arrive and get Jimmy to the County Hospital. It was after he had phoned the ambulance that Clyde had reluctantly dialled Jimmy's Dad to inform him what had happened, he in turn, phoned Donal. Patrick arrived at the site as the ambulance men carried Jimmy out strapped to a stretcher. Seeing that Jimmy was in good hands, he organised to meet him at the hospital.

Donal arrived 2 minutes later and joined the other two men. "What happened Clyde?" Patrick demanded.

"I'm sorry," said Clyde "Jimmy must have followed me here." He handed the blood stained cement bag over. "We are getting nowhere. Somehow the bastard has gotten onto me, he was waiting here for me tonight, and he was expecting me to be here. I seriously underestimated him." said Clyde as the ambulance pulled away.

"I'll see you at the hospital, Patrick." and with that he turned on his heels and walked quickly to his car.

The doctors operated on Jimmy immediately. The bullet had just missed his heart, but it had damaged much tissue and his chest cavity had to be opened up for the damage to be repaired. One lung was partially collapsed, this had to be drained. For 4 hours the surgeons cut and cleaned, finally removing the sternum clamps and stitching him up again.

Patrick and Clyde paced restlessly outside the No.2 operating theatre. Patrick would not blame Clyde; he knew his son's obsession. Looking now at Clyde, he could see why the lad adored him; tall, lean black short curly hair and he walked with a fluid cat-like grace. Patrick liked him himself. He stopped pacing now and faced Clyde. "What now?" he asked, "Where do you go from here?"

Clyde looked Patrick straight in the eyes, "I neither saw nor heard the man." he said. "On the other hand, I don't think he saw me either so we are still strangers. As soon as I find out how Jimmy is I have to go and seek him out."

"South?" Patrick enquired.

Clyde nodded. "South!" he confirmed.

"Be careful," he said with real concern, "and keep in touch."

CHAPTER 17

ODFREY DELL WAS THE PRISON Chaplin, of St Mary's Parish which was located adjacent to the prison and traditionally housed the incumbent, whose living included looking after the men's spiritual welfare.

He was a tall thin man, with a large nose and prominent adams apple which bobbed up and down agitatedly when he talked. Adenoids caused a permanent nasal problem for him and a wet handkerchief was frequently pressed to his frequently and violently blown nose. Even with this constant attention, a dew drop constantly appeared at the end of Godfrey's large red nose.

Having been born with a low sex drive, females did not, as with normal males, present him with desires. As with all asexual males, at first he found he preferred male company because interrelationships with females are almost always sexual, he had nothing to communicate with them.

After several attempts at normality, which all ended in frustrated failure, Godfrey entered ecumenical college at Bromley, supported by his widowed mother and two fairly wealthy aunts. It took 4 years at Bromley before he was ordained as curate at Lincoln. It was here, as curate in 1982, that he met Algenon Godleman. Algenon was a high profile American Evangelist on a crusade for the Lord, gathering converts like harvesting wheat.

In the huge marquee the PA system magnified Algenon's magnificent voice, charged with emotion, urging his enraptured audience to allow the light of the Lord to enter into their darkness. "Open your hearts and minds to the light and I guarantee fulfillment." he boomed. The emotion created in the marquee atmosphere was all embracing as the 750 or so potential and existing Christians swayed, holding their hands palm up to the roof. "Yes, yes, yes." they chanted.

His nose wet and his forehead damp, Godfrey allowed his very soul to become part of the emotional turmoil. In all his time in search for God, nothing had ever even remotely prepared him for this. He could feel, touch and taste Christ. "Christ the Lord, Christ the light, the power the essence of everything. He came on earth to free you. Allow him in, live in him, through him, with him, he is the Lord." the voice waded in awe-inspiring proportions. The swaying audience now almost in a trance-like daze, "Yes, yes, we feel him." they chanted. Several had been overcome and were being helped to the clear space at the back of the large tent by 'Christ's soldiers', as Algenon referred to his helpers.

At the front of the mass, a strange noise rose above the level of voices, which resembled a constant gabble of unintelligent chanting. The Lord said and my people shall speak in tongues. The born again converts of previous harvests began to pray to the Lord in Tongues.

Godfrey, in the midst of this ecstasy, suddenly realized that another phenomenon had happened. In all his 27 years, he had never had a full erection. Now, to his utter amazement, the front of his black trousers was forced out by a huge erection. Proof indeed of the Lord's power, he thought.

From that moment, Godfrey was a changed person. He shone with an inner light, fully convinced that he had now been called by the Lord. The jail was his private fishing ground, filled with specimen fish, for him to gather in the Lord's larder. Every new prisoner, regardless of religious learning, had an interview with the Reverend Godfrey. This was not normal in prison routine; however the governor was a full blown 'Born Again Christian' and shared Rev. Godfrey's desire for converts. Indeed, some of the men entering jail for the first time were ripe for Godfrey's fervor. Bewildered and ashamed, his offer of salvation was readily accepted, and he made a good harvest of these men on the rebound.

Others had been through it all before many times, these told him to frig off as soon as he approached them. His biggest challenge came from men like Bernard, low IQ, sly men looking for an excuse to strike, perhaps a release from the strict routine of prison life. Bernard had, at first, accepted Godfrey's approaches, until he realized that he gained nothing from it in the way of perks, then he too told Godfrey to 'frig off'.

Rev. Godfrey found Bernard's case strangely compelling, a violent man with obvious sexual undertow being castrated offered a unique opportunity, not only to gather in another sinner, but to investigate what effect the removal of the testicles did to a man's attitude to the Lord. A man with not balls, a shiver ran down Rev. Godfrey's spine. He felt an erection coming on and went down on his knees to pray for the Lords' forgiveness.

Bernard lay on his bed with his hands behind his head. It was three weeks now since the final operation to remove his testicles. The doctor had just removed the last of the stitches. Bernard looked down and his genital area, still dark blue and purple from Franks debilitating crush and the surgeons knife. His penis looked obscene, lying serenely without its attendant scrotum. Turmoil filled his mind.

"Hello Bernard, how are you feeling?" The voice startled him, lost in his own thoughts. He looked around blandly at Rev. Godfrey who was holding his wet hanky to his red nose blowing it loudly.

Bernard was about to tell him he wasn't interested in the Lord and being born again, when a thought struck him. Perhaps he could use the vicar in some way to solve his problem with Belinda.

In his last letter to Belinda, Bernard had asked her to visit him. A fact he had forgotten while consumed with his other problems. He was allowed one visit per month; the next time was in three weeks. "To tell you the truth Reverend, I need to talk to someone." Godfrey's adams apple bobbed up and down and his mouth opened, exposing the large horsey teeth, he gave a 'winning' smile, "The Lord be praised" he said silently to himself. Bernard then told the Reverend about the letters he had been receiving.

CHAPTER 18

J ACK LAY DOWN ON THE massage table. Belinda poured oil onto her hands and then rubbed them together. He closed his eyes as she slowly slid her oily hands over his shoulders, down his back, kneading and massaging each joint in his back, over his buttocks, down the cheeks, onto his inner thighs, down the back of his legs, kneading his calves and ankles, each leg in turn. Belinda knew her job. Back up she went, retracing the path her hands had made the first time, shoulders, neck……… "OK Johnny, turn over now." He turned over and placed his hands behind his head. She looked at his flaccid penis as she poured more oil onto her hands. "That's no good," she said in mock disapproval, "no good at all. You're not concentrating. He's normally stood up by now."

Slowly she opened the buttons of her tunic down to her waist, her large firm breasts swinging out as she took off each shoulder and pulled out her arms. As the tunic fell around her ankles, she took off her small G-string. "That's more like it!" she said as he slowly began to get aroused. "Do you want ride-a-cock-horse today Johnny?" she asked. Jack nodded.

She threw her leg over the bed and sat, slowly astride him. The massage table began so squeak as she did a ride-a-cock-horse. The music played 'Hey Jude' and then 'Green Sleeves', the bed went squeakity scratch, scratchity squeak, faster and faster then slowed until it finally stopped. The music played 'The Green Green Grass of Home'.

They sat together in the Sauna; the sweat appeared on her brown tanned body in fat droplets and dripped onto the wooden slats. Jack looked at her. She was very attractive with bright blue eyes and a wide generous mouth over large white teeth; one was chipped which made her seem even more attractive. She was evenly tanned all over from the sun-bed, her forehead and nose were heavily covered in freckles. She closed her eyes and lay back on a large white towel. Jack leaned over and kissed her on the cheek; she opened her eyes and smiled at him. Leaning towards him she ruffled his hair and her breasts jiggled.

"How would you like to earn a couple of hundred Belinda? he asked smiling.

CHAPTER 19

Belinda got out of the taxi, around the corner from the front entrance to Wakefield Prison. She walked the 300 yards to the door. She wore her white bleached hair pulled in great loops on top of her head. The bright red lipstick clashed with the pink dress, the front of which was white lace showing her ample cleavage. Her long legs were clearly visible to the thigh through the split up the side. A plastic leopard skin coat hung over her shoulders reaching down to just below her calves. Five inch high green plastic stiletto shoes completed her eye catching ensemble. A powerful cheap perfume wafted after has as she pushed her way through the main door.

A warder, sitting at the desk behind the glass screen, looked at Belinda and managed to stifle a giggle. "Bernard McIvor?" he questioned, with a strain to disguise the laughter in his voice. "Bernard McIvor?" he said again.

"Yes." she studied the warder and asked "Is there anything wrong?"

The warder could hold it in no longer and the bottled up laughter burst out of him. Belinda began to feel that the 300 pound she had extracted from Jack was not enough.

"I'm sorry" he said, wiping the tears from his eyes. "I shouldn't have laughed like that." But before he could contain it, the laughter burst from him again. When he eventually recovered his composure he said "I'm sorry, are you his girlfriend?"

"Yes" said Belinda.

"Well, he's in the prison hospital. The prison vicar would like a word with you before you see him if that's OK".

A little stuck for words "Oh, OK." she said lamely. He turned away as another fit of laughter shook him. Belinda was taken to a cream painted room with a green metal topped table in the middle.

Moments after she was seated Rev. Godfrey entered, clamping the soggy handkerchief to his red nose blowing loudly. He sat down at the table opposite her.

"My dear girl, Bernard has asked me to speak with you before seeing him" he started, "I have some good new and some bad news. The bad new is that Bernard has had both his testicles removed." Belinda stared at the vicar and noticed his adams apple bobbing up and down rapidly. She started to giggle nervously, and almost without thinking said, "And the good news?"

Somewhat taken aback by her amusement, Rev. Godfrey stared at her for a long moment before replying, "Brother Bernard has seen the light of Christ the Lord and has been born again in the name of Jesus – Hallelujah!" He reached across the table and grasped her vermillion nailed hands in this own clammy hands, "Come my dear," he said earnestly, "join with me and give thanks to the Lord for Brother Bernard's joyous enlightenment."

At this point Belinda's nerves cracked. She wrenched back her hands from his clammy grasp. Standing up rapidly, knocking over the chair in the process, she turned to the door and banged frantically, "Let me out," she shouted "let me out." A warder opened the door. "Jesus Christ," she exclaimed, "get me out of this frigging nut house."

"I never even got to see the bastard, Jack," she explained, "some lunatic vicar told me that he had died when they cut his balls off and was born again or something. If you want to know anything more, you'd better get someone else, I'm not going there again and that's final." It seemed that for the present Jack had come to a dead end.

CHAPTER 20

Rev. Godfrey Dell blew his nose loudly; the wind blew his long black cloak round his legs as he hurried across the open grass area in front of the prison officer's houses. Crossing the side road, under the high grim stone walls of the prison building, he looked up into the grey sky. The first snow flakes settled softly on his sleeve, the snow is early he thought as he approached the personnel gate, in the massive double wooden doors, and pressed the bell.

Inside the reception area, the central heating system kept the temperature at a steady 62 degrees F, today was Wednesday, official day for Rev. Godfrey to interview the weeks intake of new prisoners. The officer in the reception area caught him straight away, "Oh! Prisoner Bernard McIvor has especially requested to see you today Rev." he said.

The Rev blew his nose again, "Very well, I'll see him first – could you arrange for me to see him now please?" he asked of the officer.

"Right you are Reverend." the warder replied. Bernard 'The Enoch' as he was vulgarly called by the whole of the prison staff was well known to all; not many inmates have their balls removed in Wakefield Prison. Pushing a key on the console in front of him "Hello, level 3." a metallic voice came through a microphone, "Could you bring up 'The Enoch' George to the interview room please."

"Right you are Same." the tinny voice replied.

"He'll be up in a sec Rev." the warder said.

Godfrey sat at the green Formica topped table, "Sit down Brother Bernard." he gave Bernard one of his winning smiles showing his large yellowing horsey teeth. "What can I do for you?" he asked as he clamped his wet hanky to his nose and blew loudly.

Bernard pulled out one of the perfumed letters and placed it on front of Godfrey. Godfrey looked at the yellow letter, then at Bernard's pasty face quizzically.

"Read it." Bernard instructed. Godfrey picked up the single yellow page and read the contents:-

Darling Bernard,

Please do not worry about not being able to perform!
I fully understand and still want to remain your girl.
Have you any idea when you will be out yet? Let me
know as soon as possible.

> *Your ever loving,*
> *Belinda.*

Godfrey re-read the neat round handwriting; in his mind he could see the bleached hair and the deep mysterious cleavage of the girl called Belinda he had met once before. He looked up at Bernard expectantly.

"Can you go and see her for me and explain that when I get out I am going to help with the Lords work?" asked Bernard. Inside his own mind, great changes were taking place for Bernard as the body adapted to its new status; chemicals which affected his personality no longer were being produced, hormones and secretions kept in balance by his body's chemistry were now rearranging themselves. His blond lank hair had started to fall out and was not being replaced, his beard growth had slowed down and the hair had grown softer until it was just down like a young boys. He had started to have his hair cropped every week and the prison hairdresser, somehow the normally craggy features of his face had softened and his skin looked softer and smoother, most of the hair on his arms, once blonde and curly, had gone and his arms were white, the tattoo 'Bernard' looked obscene; his hands were white, hairless and strangely feminine.

Rev. Godfrey was worried. He looked at Bernard and an involuntary shudder ran down his spine, the changes taking place were starting to become noticeable. It had been several weeks since he had agreed to help Bernard to become one of Christ's soldiers. He returned his gaze to the letter; the address at the top was 3 Vallow Lane, Highthorne, Barrowgate, a town about 15 miles away from Wakefield.

"Please Reverend," Bernard pleaded, "I'm up for parole in a months time and I want this sorted out before then." Bernard reasoned that whoever was behind the letters, which now held no sexual attraction at all for him, could easily check up with the authorities when he was to be released. He wanted to find out as much background as possible before deciding what action to take. He only had Reverend Godfrey's description of Belinda from her brief visit as tangible evidence of the whole strange business regarding the letters.

Godfrey looked across again at the un-wholesome person sitting facing him. "Yes, leave it to me, I'll do what I can." he said resignedly.

Godfrey walked quickly along Station Road; he had requested directions from a postman a few yards from the railway station entrance. "It's a small back lane of Station Road on the right going toward the war memorial, right beside Wilson's Chemist" he had told Godfrey. As he approached the Chemist shop he saw the sign 'Vallow Lane' just above the eaves on the red brickwork of the building. He turned into it and a few yards down from the chemist window was a dark green door with a letter box, almost at ground level, a No3 on a plastic sign was fixed to the door frame. Godfrey knocked on the door and stepped back to look up at the brick building. A small window just to the left of the door, about 10' up, was obviously a stair landing. Faded net curtains hung at this window and a vase with faded pink plastic flowers stood on the window ledge. After a while, he knocked again – still nothing – self-consciously he looked up the narrow lane where he noticed an old Ford Cortina parked slightly ahead of where he stood, on the opposite side. The lane turned to the left just beyond the car but to that point, the lane was empty. He bent down and pushed the letter box. From this position he could not see through, another self-conscious look around, he got down on his hands and knees pushing the aluminium flap open. Peering through, he could see that the door led to a little lobby with stairs going up to the right. The floor was blue vinyl tiles – clean and polished – nothing else, none of the usual give away leaflets and newspaper's pushed through by unenthusiastic delivery boys eager to get rid of the load of freebies.

So absorbed, he hadn't noticed anyone coming toward him, until he felt a wet nose on his neck, "Eh up vicar, what's tha praying there for?" The voice came from an elderly man who was walking his small terrier dog down from the main road. The man looked down at Godfrey with an amused smile on his face.

Feeling extremely stupid, Godfrey hastened to stand, his face now bright red, he fished out his hanky and blew his nose, "I was, I was….." he blustered.

"It's all reet vicar tha don't ev to explain to me tha knows. If t Lord wants thee to pray on t street its nowt to do wi any bugger else." he said bursting into peals of laughter.

"No no, I was trying to look through the letter box." a flustered Godfrey blurted out.

"Oh! Peeping through letter box aye vicar, why?" he grinned.

"To see if there was anybody in."

"Well, why doesn't tha knock like any other bugger?"

Godfrey was desperate, he had got himself into a ridiculous situation, it was like a comedy farce, "I did knock," he said, "there was no reply."

"Well perhaps there is no bugger in." persisted the man.

"Yes, yes, well thank you." mumbled Godfrey and rushed of towards the main road. At Station Road he turned left and walked past Wilson's chemist shop, the little man followed him, obviously enjoying Godfrey's discomfort. The dog barked excitedly as if he too was enjoying the change in routine.

"Oh Lord." said Godfrey as he saw the man and dog turning out of Vallow Lane. Desperately he looked for some escape as the irritating little man and his barking dog were closing in on him. A woman came out of Wilson's, and on impulse, Godfrey caught the closing door and went in. The shop was the old fashioned type without selling shelves and gondolier's, the small shop was empty and at the far end was the counter, in front of a small dispensary. An attractive girl stood behind the counter wearing a white uniform, she smiled at Godfrey. "May I help you?" she asked pleasantly.

"Oh, err, err." Godfrey pulled out his hanky and blew a loud blast from his nose. Sally Brown, the assistant, felt his embarrassment and he blew his nose again. Now, almost purple in the face, he could register nothing, tongue tied and speechless, he hid behind his wet handkerchief.

Sally, who was a product of the 60's, had run across this problem before, only with teenagers. "Don't worry vicar, they are over here." she said trying to put him at ease as she indicated a large display of condoms at the end of the counter.

At this, Godfrey began to cough uncontrollably. Fearing he would choke, Sally called to Jack who was in the dispensary. He raced out and pulled a small cane chair from the corner and placed it behind Godfrey. "Here, sit down and try to relax." he told Godfrey. With that he went back to the dispensary and returned a few moments later with a small plastic cup full of white liquid. "Here," he told Godfrey, "drink this."

Godfrey had by now recovered slightly and was able to swallow the liquid, "Oh my work, how embarrassing." he said. "I'm so sorry to cause such a fuss."

"No problem vicar." replied Jack. "Was there something we can help you with, I'm sure Sally didn't mean to be facetious." and he glared at Sally who grinned back at him.

"No, not really, I only came in on" his voice tailed away, with an effort he marshaled his thoughts, "I actually came in to enquire whether or not you know anything about the flat out the back, No 3 Vallow Lane?"

Jack started, could it be; Belinda's words flashed across his mind 'some lunatic vicar' she had said. He glared again at Sally and she retreated back to the counter. "What did you want to know vicar?" he asked as casually as he could.

"Do you know who lives there?" Godfrey asked.

"Actually, I own the property so yes I do know who lives there." said Jack. "Perhaps you would be more comfortable in my office," he continued leading Godfrey towards a door at the side of the counter, "come this way." He held the door open and Godfrey walked through.

Godfrey was now seated in a leather arm chair with a cup of strong black coffee. "Now vicar, what was it you were wanting to know?" Jack said carefully.

"I'm trying to contact a girl called Belinda, who I'm led to believe lives at No3, on behalf of one of my flock." Jack's mind raced, so this was the lunatic vicar and McIvor was one of his flock.

"It's rented to a Mrs. Dunbar." said Jack." I very rarely see here, she goes out early morning and comes back late at night."

"Would she be called Belinda, I wonder?" said Godfrey. "What does she look like?"

Jack had hooked his fish after all, now he didn't know whether he should play it, or cut the line; then an idea came to him.

"What does Belinda look like vicar?" countered Jack.

"Blonde hair, very noticeable clothes, about 30ish." said Godfrey.

"Ah! That's not Mrs. Dunbar. It would be her friend who looks like that, but she doesn't live at No3."

"Oh," said Godfrey at a bit of a loss, "you wouldn't know how I could contact her, would you?"

"I'm afraid not," Jack sympathized, "perhaps you could give me the message and I'll try and get in contact with Mrs. Dunbar and have her pass the message to her friend.

"It is a little complicated." hesitated Godfrey.

"Well if you want to give me your details, I might be able to get her to contact you." Jack said, in an attempt to gain Godfrey's confidence.

Godfrey thought for a moment, "No, I'll explain it to you; it may prove to be the best way to get the message delivered." He drew a deep breath and began. "Bernard, one of my flock, has been born again and is looking to join God's army as one of Christ's Soldiers. To do so he must renounce the sins of the flesh and take up the Banner of Christ, pure and un-sullied, like all of Christ's soldiers he must be prepared to answer the call and join the pure in heart and mind. Think pure, be pure, is our motto." Godfrey's fervor had produced a rash of sweat beads on his upper lip and forehead, with his damp hanky he wiped off the sweat, blowing his nose loudly afterwards. Then he continued, "To accomplish this he must reconcile himself to forsaking worldly pleasure's, this he is prepared to do, made considerably easier since having his testicles removed due to an accident. However, his task is complicated by his past."

"I'll bet it is!" thought Jack.

"This girl Belinda has so far not accepted Brother Bernard's glorious admission into Christ's Church; she has persisted in her attempts to entangle Bernard in her sexual and unacceptable behaviour. He has asked me to seek her out again and speak with her on his behalf; I met her once in prison but could not convince her then to stay away."

Jack stared blankly at the perspiring vicar, his mind racing, so the murderous twisted bastard had thrown in with the 'God Squad' he thought. Clearing his throat, he stood and walked to the small window overlooking the backyard, "The only time I see Mrs. Dunbar is the last Friday of the month when she pays her rent, so that will be two week away."

"Brother Bernard could be out in 10 days time," Godfrey said, "so we will have to pray to the Lord that we can help him overcome his past and go forth in the glory of god."

'Amen' to that thought Jack; I'll send the bastard off to meet the Lord in person. He turned to Godfrey, "Leave it to me vicar, I'll contact Mrs. Dunbar and get the message through to Belinda."

Godfrey did not fully relate his accounts to Bernard; firstly he did not tell him that Belinda did not actually live at 3 Vallow Lane, neither did he tell him that he had left the message with the chemist; all he assured Bernard was that he did not think that he would get any further contact with Belinda. So the letter which Bernard received two days later came as somewhat of a shock:

> *Murderer!*
> *I know you did it, you killed her, I know you are*
> *getting out in a few days time. Now you are going to*

pay. Meet me at the flat at 9:00pm on Friday 15th
December. Don't tell that lunatic vicar or I'll put you
back in jail for life.

Bernard had his last prison hair cut at 4:15pm on Tuesday afternoon. At 8:30am on the Wednesday the prison rehabilitation society had given him 125 pounds. Brother Bernard, 'The Enoch', was released on parole on Wednesday 13th December at 9:00am.

CHAPTER 21

A T 8:00PM ON FRIDAY THE 15ᵗʰ December, a tall blonde woman wearing a grey raincoat turned from Station Road into Vallow Lane, walking quickly, with big long strides, she went straight past No. 3. At the end of the brick building was a small patch of grass fenced off from the rear property; a small courtyard to the right was fenced off from the grass parking area. The blonde moved quickly into the shadows at the rear of the grassed area and stood behind the dustbins in the shadow of the overgrown privet hedge. In the small, dimly lit courtyard, there were two doors; one leading to the rear of the chemist, the other to a toilet. A fire escape led up to another door at the first floor level, the whole building was in darkness.

After checking her surroundings, the woman walked quickly to the fence, placing a gloved hand on the gate post, she vaulted over and made her way up the fire escape, pausing on the landing to listen; at the top she looked down into the deserted courtyard. She produced a tyre lever from her coat pocket, forcing it between the jamb and the door, she levered the door open. The Yale lock sprang off with a splintering sound; checking to make sure nobody had heard, she went inside and closed the door behind her.

With the money received from the prison, Bernard had bought a blond wig, grey mackintosh and brown shoes for 25pound from the Oxfam shop, the dress he had stolen from the launderette, another 5pound bought him cheap eye shadow, foundation and lipstick, the gloves he had struck lucky with as they were in a pocket of the Oxfam coat; strangely he felt at home in women's clothes.

Satisfied he hadn't been seen, Bernard looked around the kitchen, it was completely empty, nothing; the cable from the cooker hung down from the switch box. Quickly he crossed to the door, the room beyond was also empty; bare floor boards, he didn't understand, how could the flat be empty. The lounge was darker that the kitchen, heavy curtains hung at the window, Bernard carefully placed a foot into the room, he could smell something funny, a bit like being in a dentists surgery. Quietly he walked across to the door at the opposite end, he paused and sniffed again, what was that smell? It was stronger at this end of the room.

CHAPTER 22

J ACK HAD TAKEN A BOTTLE of chloroform from the stock room, together with a cotton wool pack. Although he had never expected Bernard to arrive early, he had gone upstairs at 8:00pm to be sure he was prepared. Standing alone in the empty flat he had gone over his plan in his mind.

He was now standing behind the curtains, hardly daring to breathe. When the lock broke on the back kitchen door, he had been looking down Vallow Lane towards Station Road; the only person he had seen was the blonde, but he had only paid her slight attention as he was expecting a man – Bernard.

Now that someone was breaking in his first reaction was to stay hidden. The flat was empty and he had intended to catch Bernard by surprise downstairs in the small hall. Jack was not a quick thinker; his methodical brain needed time to place thins in the correct order. Now his mind was in turmoil. His hand still held the curtains open a crack, peering out, and he quickly stepped back into the window space. In his haste, he knocked over the bottle of chloroform, the liquid slowly leaked out of the top which he had not screwed tightly enough shut.

From his hiding place Jack watched the figure enter the kitchen, slowly, cautiously. Startled he realized it was the blond woman. He was starting to feel faint from the fumes leaking into the space between the window and the curtain.

As Bernard approached the curtains the strong chloroform smell had started to unnerve him. Then from the darkened room he heard a groan and the curtains gave way; Jack had collapsed and rolled onto the floor at his feet. Something in him snapped, in a blind panic he turned and fled back through the kitchen and down the back stairs.

CHAPTER 23

A FTER HIS COLLAPSE JACK HAD come round to find himself alone in the flat. Feeling rather foolish, he pulled himself into a sitting position and took stock of the situation. He mentally processed what had happened. He was convinced that Bernard had raped and killed his helpless daughter, but was that good enough? He had no proof. Even to him it wasn't enough, he had to prove to himself that Bernard did it.

He had intended to force the truth out of Bernard once he had overcome him with chloroform. Now he had to admit that this wasn't practical, he wasn't up to this kind of behaviour. But what was the next step? To locate Bernard again, the whole Belinda and flat ideas was of no use now and Bernard had probably seen his face, in fact he was lucky to have been left in one piece.

The next day he obtained Godfrey's telephone number from the jail and phoned. "Oh, Good morning Reverend, this is Jack Wilson, do you remember me? I own the flat in Vallow Lane."

"Yes, yes, I remember," said Godfrey, "what can I do for you?"

"You asked me to get in touch with Belinda, and I'm sorry it took so long but I have reached her."

"Oh, thank you anyway," said Godfrey, "but I don't think it matters now. Brother Bernard left this morning with the New Army of God touring America, but I certainly appreciate you ringing back."

Jack sat back in his chair with a sigh and replaced the phone. It took him nearly the whole day to establish the New Army of God's timetable in America. Finally he got through to the Free Church of God Revival Center in Campden Town, north of London. The woman who answered the phone was most helpful; she explained to Jack that although there could be minor changes to the schedule, that the New Army of God and its driving force, Algernon Godleman would be in Boston for the next 3 months. From there they would move onto Washington where they would stay for 6 months. After that it was 2 months in Philadelphia or 3 months in New Orleans, this was yet to be decided.

Jack could easily justify a trip to the States, most of the large drug companies in America put on seminars for new drug releases. All Jack had to do was run through the massive piles of literature put out by the drug companies to find a seminar that was to be held in Boston during the next 3 months.

CHAPTER 24

STUART JONES WAS BORN IN 1943 in a small town in Pennsylvania called Horizon. His father had died when he was two and his mother had kept him, as best she could, on state welfare and the few dollars she made by cleaning for a wealthy family in town.

Stuart was different from the other boys of his age. At sixteen all the boys in his year at High School could talk about was girls and sex. He could not understand their preoccupation with females – "I actually stuck my finger up her in class." he heard one of the boys telling his friends in the toilet. "Right under the teachers nose and she didn't even notice." he told them gleefully. "I was on my hand and knees under the desk and she just sat there with her legs open, pretending to work." He held out his finger, "Here, smell this!" "Wow".

He left Horizon High School with reasonable graduation marks, but no firm idea of what to do with the rest of his life. In the local paper had been an advertisement 'Young bright people with will to succeed required, full training given and must be prepared to travel. All those interested come to the New Star Motel, Grange Street at 6:30pm Wed, Thurs and Fri 26th, 27th & 28th July for further details'.

In the function room of the hotel on the Wednesday night about 25 youngish people sat waiting. Upon the raised stage, where every Saturday night 'Smokey Joe and the Rio combination' played music while the townsfolk danced, two men and a woman sat at a table.

The man in the centre took a drink from a glass, cleared his throat and stood up. "Good evening," he said, "thank you all for coming."

The company was recruiting for salesmen to travel America selling 'The Good News Bible' door to door and through Gospel meetings held along the route. Stuart was at 18, tall, well built and extremely handsome. In fact, he was perfect material for 'The Good News' team; good, clean looking, fresh and wholesome. After the meeting he was accepted for training; three months at the 'Good News Centre' in Washington. The Good News organization was slick, professional and highly successful. The personnel running the training school rejected 60% of the hopeful recruits after the first day sending them home with an apology and $20. Of the remaining 40% only 5% finished the full three months and joined the rolling band wagon spreading the light and selling the written word of the Lord.

Algernon Godleman was a salesman for McGiver Creek Silk Handkerchiefs, a big man with a shock of dark wavy hair. He had a set round which he serviced which covered 300 miles of territory, servicing his customers each 3 times a year. Algernon was a homosexual, his wife and two children totally unaware of his disposition. At home, most week-ends, he was a normal husband and father, performing and fulfilling his role in the leafy suburb. His wife Louise was quite content with his performance, not every week-end but 2 or 3 times a month he would climb on top and grunt a few times before rolling over to sleep.

At 20, Stuart Jones was well established in the Good News team. As yet he had not been given publicity and full stage exposure, but the organization had an eye on him as a top potential money spinner – big and powerful. They had coached him in speaking, his powerful modulated voice was rich and compelling, his future was certain.

Within the travelling circus of bible selling and purveyors of light and goodness, and beneath the surface of fresh air and wholesomeness, lurked the perversion, corruption and greed that vast sums of money always bred and nurtured.

Endless streams of ordinary, honest people poured their money into Good News coffers, frightened by the constant bombardment from the news media of drugs, murder and violence, troubled by the imagined breakdown or moral standards and desperately searching for some reassurance and hope for their salvation. On the constantly returning circuit every 6 months, the team returned to revitalize the campaign, reaping more and more converts who had 'seen the light' and relieved their burden of guilt by emptying their bank accounts.

Stuart was being paid well for his work and all his living expenses were paid for, good and reasonable motel accommodation, he was starting to enjoy the status.

The team had arrived at Hardonton, a small town in Georgia, and they had booked into the Eastfield Motel. The marquee had been erected and ready for the first performance the next day. Stuart was sitting in the lounge reading a magazine, finishing his coffee after dinner, when a large well built man walked into the lounge and sat in the chair facing him. He folded his paper and smiled at Stuart. "Hello," he said as he extended his hand toward Stuart, "Algernon."

"Hi' said Stuart, "I'm Stuart."

"Pleased to meet you Stuart, care for a drink?"

Not normally a drinker he was about to say no, but then, "Yes, thank you, I will."

"Waiter." called Algernon. As they waiter approached "Jack Daniels for me" he said.

"And?" he looked to Stuart.

"Oh, err, the same please."

"Bring us the bottle." Algernon said before the waiter had a chance to walk away.

"Yes Sir."

Stuart didn't try to determine why he liked this man, this total stranger, but he felt unreasonably at ease with him. They talked about each others likes and dislikes, tastes and many other normal topics, the level of the bottle continuing to fall until it was empty. By now it was late and the hotel was nearly empty, most of the guests having returned to their rooms. "I have another bottle in my room." said Algernon. "Care to join me?" Without hesitation Stuart agreed. He felt flushed and excited and his breath was catching in his throat. As he followed Algernon into his room, he looked around the deserted grounds furtively, and then closed the door behind them.

CHAPTER 25

THE GOOD NEWS TEAM VISITED Hardonton every six months, Algernon every three. Stuart and Algernon left messages for one another regarding dates when they would next be there. The giving and receiving of the piece in 90% of homosexual relationships relates to the constant reversal of roles from giving to receiving.

A report published in the Cleveland Echo by the Hillington Research Foundation of Ohio stated that because of lack of fundamental stability within homosexual behaviour a fluctuating imbalance of hormonal changes forced 90% of all homosexuals to play different roles to experience any form of satisfaction. Giving today, receiving tomorrow. Stuart however was one of the 10%. A stabilized 'giver', his complete satisfaction came from his role as a dominant personality in the relationship.

It was late on Thursday night that he retired with Algernon to room 306. This was the third time they had met up since their initial meeting. Stuart however had seduced 1 or 2 of the weaker members of the team, so he was 'giving' regularly when on the road with the team. After a certain amount of foreplay, centered mainly on the Vaseline jar which Algernon carried in his overnight case, Stuart was straining to give a good performance. His eyes tightly shut and the veins bunched beneath the skin of his neck, slowly he built up the pressure, his fingers gripped the muscles of Algernon's upper thighs, he became aware of a shudder and a relaxing of the object of his giving. There was a long sigh and suddenly the set up collapsed and Stuart fell onto the bed, the muscular control which had supported him during his efforts to reach for hold no longer existed. He looked at Algernon's face, it was blue and through his pouted lips tiny bubbles of mucus slowly emerged. He was obviously going through the stages of a massive heart attack. Stuart's first reaction was to run and shout for help. He leapt from the bed and ran to the door, at the door he paused – naked – and looked back at the bed where Algernon lay, also naked with his long legs spread eagled. Slowly he returned to the bed, sure the man was already gone, he felt for the pulse at the side of his neck, nothing. He sat in the arm chair staring at Algernon.

After a long while, he stood and put on his clothes. He folded Algernon's clothes and hung them in the wardrobe. On the writing desk lay his wallet and a gold omega watch. He picked up the wallet and opened it, inside was several credit cards and $325 cash. Going to his overnight bag, he found a leather case which contained several documents including his passport, driving licence and birth certificate. He put them back where he found them.

Returning to the bed, he moved Algernon to a more natural position in the bed and covered him with the bed covers. With a last look around the room to ensure that it looked normal, Stuart left through the glass doors at the rear. Closing the doors quietly behind him, he returned to his own room. The motel grounds were deserted and he was not seen.

Stuart never really understood what had made him keep Algernon's personal documents, but within two months they had become part of an elaborate plan to change Stuart into one of the most popular charismatic and wealthy perverts in the world wide 'Search for truth through the Lords movement'.

The team had moved on the next morning. Algernon was found at 10:30am and the police were at a loss to explain why certain were missing (not aware obviously of the other documents) but his wallet with his money and credit cards. A verdict was given of death by massive coronary cardiac arrest, that pathologist, although aware of homosexual behaviour, did not think it prudent to mention it in the autopsy report. Algernon's death passed into history. Louise collected $300,000 from North Star Assurance and $75,000 from McGiver Creek, thankful for his prudence in taking out life assurance as well as that given by the company he had worked for.

CHAPTER 26

STUART'S MOTHER HAD DIED WHEN he was 19 and apart from the team, he had no relations or friends. Going through Algernon's papers, he was pleased to find a complete identity consisting of Birth Certificate, Passport, drivers licence and credit cards. The credit cards would be cancelled of course but they would save as proof of identity should the occasion arise.

One of the powerful of the sleeping committee of Good Life was Pamela Lea, the wife of Marshall Lea. He was the director, taking no part in the front end of the band wagon. He took the contributions and bible sales money and converted the burgeoning stream into an extremely healthy bank balance for the shareholders. Marshall was a tall, dried up stick of a man. Pamela was a lush, needing and taking sexual pleasures whenever and wherever she could. She could not however, tempt Stuart into any situation no matter how hard she tried. She was to find out the reason for this when returning to the marquee one evening to retrieve her handbag from the hospitality lounge located at the rear of the stage. In the darkened marquee she could hear sounds, scuffling noises coming from the rear of the stage. Fuelled by her many bourbons, she silently moved toward the rear of the stage. The flap, which served as a door, was closed and the light was off but she could hear that someone was definitely in the room. The street light from the nearby road provided sufficient light to establish that two people were indulging in some form of deviation.

Pamela, now fully prepared to rush in indignantly, quietly reached for the light switch. 'Click' and the light flooded the small room and she swept back the door. 'My God', she breathed, Stuart was 'giving' Ian Jackson. Ian was bent over the wooden trestle which was covered in a white cloth, Stuart his black trousers around his ankles turned in horror to stare at Pamela. Unable to contain herself she burst into peals of laughter, letting the flag fall back she went quickly out of the marquee and drove away.

That very night, Stuart left town on the night sleeper as Algernon Godleman.

It was two years later when he emerged from the mid west of the new army of God, the all singing all dancing, follow me and I will show you the light of the Lord.

The new crusade rolled across America headed by its powerful preacher 'Algernon the Magnificent'.

Twenty years on, now rich beyond the dreams of avarice, Algernon sat at the window table of the New Citadel restaurant in Wakefield, Yorkshire. It was not his favourite place but the best on offer within driving distance of this part of his campaign. The chauffeur driven Rolls Royce, on hire from Ripon Bros., sat in the car park waiting to drive him back to the Post House Hotel Guisley. Reverend Godfrey Dell sat opposite him. "I'm sure he would be of great use to you in your campaign," he said, "a good example of what the Lord can achieve with a poor sinner."

"No balls you say reverend, no balls." he pondered. "Yes, I think I could use such a poor sinner if he is prepared to embrace the Lord."

"Oh, he is dedicated." said Godfrey, blowing his nose loudly.

Algernon stared into his balloon glass at the restaurants most prestigious Cognac and sipped it slowly, "Alright, have him meet me tomorrow after the morning revival meeting."

CHAPTER 27

T HE ROAD BLOCK HAD BEEN deliberately placed so that when the drivers realised it was a road block they had no other way to go but through it. The dirty yellow Toyota came around the bend, "Jesus Billy, it's the Garde, stop for Christ Sake." The car slewed to a halt with its wheel's over the pavement.

At the road block there were 15 members of the Ulster Constabulary and 10 or 12 British Soldiers. 8 of these were spread among the approach behind trees and hedges. As the yellow car braked and snaked across the road several members of Her Majesty's armed forces cocked weapons. Adrenalin pumped around their bodies. The Major in charge, using a bull horn, shouted a warning, "This is an official road block. If you are armed, throw out your weapons and get out of the vehicle with your hands on your heads."

"Billy, there's too much at stake at this time with Sean going to the Arabs next week, I'm going to try and make a break." the hoarse, barely audible, whisper rasped.

"Good luck boyo." said Billy.

Slowly and deliberately, without moving his upper body, he carefully took two grenades from a holdall on the seat beside him. "On the count of three." he said grimly. Simultaneously they opened the doors, Quiet O'Rourke on the left and Billy on the right. Slightly to the right and in front of O'Rourke was a bus shelter behind which he could see three camouflaged figures carefully placed. About 20 feet to the left of the bus shelter were another two, or perhaps three. Behind the bus shelter was a grass strip and a service road, if he could just make it to the walkway he could easily lose the army in the estate. They both swung their legs out onto the pavement. "Three." said Billy.

Billy hurled the grenade towards the three behind the bus shelter, a 2 second fuse fragmentation grenade. It blew while still in the air about 3 feet in front of the soldiers. Apart from the dreadful carnage from the 8mm think steel segments, the concussion of an explosion at close quarters is momentarily debilitating, the other 4 soldiers within 20 feet of the grenade were pushed over by the shockwave. Intent on self preservation, they fell, glad to get down for a few minutes.

From the other side of the road a battle hardened Sergeant, who had grown up in Glasgow, squeezed the trigger on his armalite gently and purposefully. Billy felt the 7.62mm bullet slam into his chest and a giant fist closed his lungs, he was prepared to die for the cause but he had not imagined anything like this pain was possible, white hot and searing his very being. In his left hand was still the other grenade he had been holding. He had pulled the pin inside the car and had started to drawback his arm to throw it across the road when he had been hit. Now only his first and second fingers held the lever against the steel body that was cut like squares of Cadbury chocolate. The pain from the bullet cut off all thoughts from his brain; nothing, nothing but this white incandescent fire in his chest. The grenade fell from his uncontrolled fingers – one, two..........oblivion.

Protected by the car, O'Rourke was thrown across the grass by the blast and fell beside the bus shelter shaken but unhurt. From his prone position he could see that the army were badly shaken, men running and shouting, the three hit but the first grenade lay sprawled and badly mutilated a few yards from the bus shelter.

The Major was running across the service road, incredibly towards O'Rourke, still holding the bullhorn. O'Rourke took aim at this mans middle with his Browning; he saw the man stumble and fall on the grass, rolling over and over in agony, the bullhorn clattered to the roadside. O'Rourke got to his knees and gathered his strength for a sprint to the service road; there were no soldiers within 20 yards of him. The grenade which had shredded Billy had started a fire in the car causing think black smoke to billow across towards the bus shelter giving O'Rourke some cover. Just then the other grenades left in the car exploded, keeping low he ran for the Alley.

In his haste, as he reached the entrance to the alley he had not seen the metal spikes concealed by the grass, the remains of a concrete post to stop motor bikes being ridden through the alley. He fell heavily to the ground breaking his right arm just below the elbow, the gun hit the asphalt and slid onto the grass, and the steel rod hooked into his leg and ripped his calf muscle. O'Rourke rolled over, cursing his bad luck. Holding his leg he tried to rise, pausing on one knee, the blood was pouring out of his gaping wound. Desperately he looked up the Alleyway, a back yard gate only 5 or 6 feet away was open, looking back he saw several soldiers were running toward him. Hopping and stumbling, he dragged himself towards the gate.

Sergeant Charlie Parker enjoyed being in the army. Most of all he liked shooting; he had always been considered the best marksman in the regiment. This earned him several contract assignments with the IRA and he was known for his cool, detached attitude towards his tasks. After shooting Billy and waiting for the second grenade blast wave to pass him, he watched O'Rourke run across the road. Calmly he centred the foresight between his shoulder blades, but just as he had gently caressed the trigger, O'Rourke had stumbled and fallen. Before he could get the armalite on him again, the smoke had obscured the alley. Running swiftly to the alley, Charlie was joined by a Lieutenant and two other soldiers. "Good shooting Sergeant." said the Lieutenant. "But listen, this one is a known important one." he laughed grimly. "Can we try and get him alive?"

The ground around the backyard gate was splattered with blood but there was no-one there. "He's badly hurt." said the Lieutenant. "Let's find him." Carefully Charlie peered around the gate post, the yard was empty. The blood trail ran beside the house between a high fence and the house end. At the front of the terraced house was a small garden, running quickly up the roadside they looked all around. Cars were parked at either side of the road but they could see nobody.

"I'll take this side, you take the other Sergeant." said the Lieutenant. "He'll not get into a house around here easily, this is protestant country." Charlie ran across the road, bending to try and look beneath the cars. The Lieutenant had only gone past two cars when he shouted, "In front, about 20 yards!"

O'Rourke ran, stumbling across the road and tripped on the curb and fell at Charlies feet. With a snarl he tried to rise. Without hesitation, Charlie kicked his broken arm. O'Rourke stifled a scream but lay still when Charlie placed the muzzle of his armalite against his temple.

CHAPTER 28

C LYDE LOOKED DOWN AT THE man on the bed; he was in the maximum security wing of the hospital section of Maze Jail. "He's heavily sedated Major." said the doctor. O'Rourke's arm was in plaster and his leg was protected by a metal cage.

"How long does the drug take to work?" he asked as the doctor prepared a syringe.

It was obvious from the expression on his face that the doctor wasn't happy. "Well it depends on the patient. I haven't had any experience of this kind of business before, I only know what I have read and that is limited to certain information obtained by the Americans in Vietnam. Apparently the relaxation of all mental inhibitions is complete for anything up to an hour, provided that post hypnotic implications have been carried out."

"Cannot the mind be controlled without the drug?" asked Clyde.

"Not in the case of such massive resistance as we have with these people."

The doctor lifted O'Rourke's left arm and holding the wrist with his thumb raised a vein in his forearm. He deftly slid the needle into the vein and pumped in 3cc's of the greenish drug irreverently called by the Americans 'The Blabber'. As the drug was carried to his brain by his blood, O'Rourke stirred and began to murmur. The doctor moved to his head and shone a small powerful beam into each of his eyes in turn, the pupil beneath the lids were almost the size of the brown smoky iris. In a strange sing-song voice the doctor started to ask questions.

Doctor: "Who are you?"

O'Rourke: "Assistant General Commander, Son's of Erin in the National Resistance Movement for the Freedom of Ireland."

Doctor: "Give me the address of your headquarters."

O'Rourke: "Flat 3 Bevlan Road, North Dublin."

Doctor: "Who is the General Commander?"

O'Rourke: "Sean McCracken."

Doctor: "Where is Sean McCracken now?"

O'Rourke: "He lives at 33 Wheaten Road, Durnal." Before the doctor could ask anymore questions, O'Rourke continued to babble, as if he wanted to help. "But he's on the Mainland now, and on Thursday he flies to Libya to discuss operation 'Burning Torch' with Hassan Gahamahl."

Doctor: "What is operation 'Burning Torch'?"

O'Rourke: "A central operating financial fund which all freedom fighters will have access to. It's formed by contributions from several wealthy states and freedom organisations which have gained government status."

His mind racing, Clyde whispered to the doctor to ask him what name McCracken would travel under.

O'Rourke: "John Page." came the reply.

Even with the British Governments lack of cooperation with Libya after the closing of the peoples Bureau in London, Sir Charles Maybury-Brown, Secretary of State for Northern Ireland, after consultations with Donal Gardner (Chief Constable of Greater Belfast) had arranged a visa for Clyde Machin of Gregory's to collect drawing and contract documents for a quotation to be prepared for a large hospital in Tripoli.

The controller at Heathrow for B.A. received a phone call on Wednesday night from the foreign office. Seat C59 was to be made available for Mr Clyde Machin on flight BA2021 on Thursday the

15th. No reason was given or requested, such things happened occasionally and were not to be explained or questioned.

As the pilot for flight BA2021 requested clearance for take off from runway 3, Sean McCracken (booked under the name of John Andrew Page) sat in seat D49 and stared out across the tarmac to the bright lights of terminal 3. Two seats behind him sat a tall hard looking man with short cropped hair and green eyes. Although the man in seat C59 knew the real identity of the man in seat D49; and the man in D49 was completely unaware of the man in C59; what neither of them knew was that Sean's father Seamus and Clyde's natural father Andrew McCracken, were brothers and that both these men on flight BA2021 flying to Tripoli had inherited Kathleen's legacy.

CHAPTER 29

KATHLEEN MCSWEENEY WAS 18 YEARS old when she married Patrick McCracken in the small Catholic Church in Ballihorrie, Southern Ireland and went on to have 5 children, raising them on their pig farm. Somewhere in her lineage was an unusual vein of extremely high IQ which seemed to hit and miss through the generations, appearing randomly. Kathleen had passed this on directly to John (her second child) and indirectly to Sean (her grandson, son of her oldest child Shamus).

* * * * * * * * * * * * * * *

Kathleen felt as if her very soul was being sucked out of her by the crude stone walls and the ever present smell of pigs emanating from the dark half circles of grimed-in pig shit on Patrick's fingers. Even a bath downstairs in the galvanized hip bath on a Saturday night with carbolic soap could not mask the smell. She was lying in the old iron bed listening to Patrick's stream of urine hitting the galvanized bucket behind the curtain in the corner of the dark bedroom waiting for what she knew was coming next. When he was done peeing he returned and climbed onto the bed. There was no pleasure for Kathleen, he simply climbed onto her and bucked and thrust into her. This unfeeling numbing routine had produced 5 children and only stopped for a few weeks before and after the birth of each baby. Earlier on in their marriage she had tried to encourage some tenderness into their relationship but that had quickly deteriorated into what she now endured nightly. With a grunt and explosion of whiskey breath he finished and wiped his pole on her flannel nightie.

As he slurped his tea from the saucer at breakfast the next morning he looked at her across the table and said "You should be missing a bleed soon, we need another boy." Kathleen smiled a wan smile; she had been taking quinine tablets for a while and had already expelled the latest fetus a few days after it was conceived. Later that day she walked to the bus top and paid for her fare to Dublin. 12 hours later she boarded a boat for America and left Ireland forever leaving Patrick McCracken with 5 children, the eldest not 7 years old. When Shamus, the youngest, was 18, Patrick died. Shamus had been feeding the pigs for 11 years now; nothing had changed now his father was dead.

Kathleen had given a legacy to John, her second born. By the candlelight, in his curtained off corner of the loft room he shared with the others of his family, John saw in the books left by his mother a different world to the peat bogs and black land of the east coast farmlands. The village school taught him to read and write only, his shrewd sharp brain did the rest.

At 17, 6 months after Shamus became owner of the farm, John left for Dublin where he married Ellen. She matched him perfectly, mouse-like, simple and a plain person as colourless as towns' water. Blindly she lay and submitted to pregnancy after pregnancy, working the land and milking the two cows, life was one long battle to stay alive. Sean was the eldest, Shirley was next. Kathleen had passed on through Shamus, her legacy of brains to Sean, endowing him with the same natural talent. His IQ, although not yet tested, was almost at the genius threshold, but in this land of complex and simple characters, nothing is straight forward. Contrasting Sean, Shirley, his sister, was severely mentally retarded. An incontinent, slavering, strange looking child with haunting dead almond shaped eyes. "She's OK." Ellen would say to the kids, "She's just a bit backward, she'll grow out of it." They treated her as normal, but to Sean it was an immense and cruel burden which was to damage his unusual intellect beyond repair! They were made to sleep in the same bed, which Shirley wet every night. Each morning Sean awoke to the ammonia stink of a urine soaked mattress, with his idiot grunting sister lolling on the pillow. Years after, he would wake up with a start in some hotel bedroom, wet with sweat, and hear laboured breathing through hereditary damaged nasal passages and smell the damp ammonia smell of that mattress.

＊＊＊＊＊＊＊＊＊＊＊＊＊＊

Father Patrick Kelly had been the priest when Kathleen had walked into the small church at Ballihorrie. What a striking woman, he thought, and his breath caught in his throat as she smiled at him. Forcing back, to the dark recesses of his mind his thoughts, he turned and walked down the aisle, but for the rest of his life that radiant smile never left him. Sometimes, on his hard bed at night, alone with God and his own thoughts, the face came back to him and swam before his closed eyes. He came regularly to visit the McCracken family, although Kathleen rarely went to church. It seemed to Father Kelly that God had sent Kathleen to test his faith; each time he saw her, his knees became weak, his stomach churned and his heart beat increased. Father Kelly, secretly, was affected far more by Kathleen's leaving than anybody else. It seemed to him that the sun had gone forever. Hiding behind his clerical mask, nobody knew how he felt except himself.

Ten years later, Father Kelly knocked at Camague House off the road to Dromade, the home of Lady Winston Atherton-Fullmark, a lady of great poise and wealth; and very attractive, even at 60. The wisened old gnome of a butler preceded him into the drawing room, "The Priest, Ma'am." he intoned.

"Come in Father." she exclaimed, "How nice of you to call. He sank into an armchair. "Tea, with a little something?" she enquired.

Father Kelly smiled, "That would be nice – keep out the damp." his eyes crinkling at the corners. Over the last few years he had a few 'little something' in his tea, beside the open log fire with Lady Winston. She rang the bell beside the fireplace, after a few minutes with no reply she stood up, "I'd better go and arrange it myself. Harrington's deafness is, as when you arrive, unusually bad." she smiled and left the room, her long tweed skirt swirling about her still attractive legs.

Father Kelly had been visiting Lady Winston now for almost fifteen years, since the death of her husband Viscount Archibald Atherton-Fullmark, the 7th Earl of Donague. He stared into the log fire, then about the room. He picked up the newspaper, 'The Boston Tribune' (an American provincial newspaper) from the mahogany side table. He had been flicking through the paper for 10 or 12 pages now without really seeing anything. However, when he reached the centre page he was completely taken up by an account of a coffee shop chain called 'Shamrock Cake & Coffee Shops'. The article announced that the chain had just opened up its 500th outlet in Canada. But the shock was not from the article, but the half page photograph of its founder – Mary O'Rourke.

When Kathleen had landed at Boston, she had already a $5000 loan from an elderly retired newspaper owner (originally an Irish immigrant), she had befriended on the voyage. He had spent a lifetime building up a chain of provincial newspapers which he had subsequently sold, his shrewd knowledge of people over his 75 years had told him Kathleen was a winner, he was correct, the loan was repaid, including a self imposed amount of interest, within 12 months. 'Shamrock Café and Coffee Shop' in Leaf Square took off from the first day and within 5 years Kathleen had 27 of these coffee shops. From this she had formed the first franchise agreements in American history selling the idea and using the Boston shop as a corporate image. The chain took off at the alarming rate of 1 opening each week.

CHAPTER 30

JOHN WAS NOW ESTABLISHED IN Dublin and as Shamus and Ellen's family grew it became more and more difficult to keep the family fed. So it was decided Sean would go to Dublin to live with his Uncle John.

Sean arrived at Dublin Central Railway Station on a Monday morning clutching a battered, cheap suitcase; he was just 12 years old. His dark curly hair raggedly cut by his mother with the kitchen scissors. He looked around the bustling crowds; he had never seen so many people. Shamus, the night before, had taken him to the railway station in the pony and cart, bought him a one way ticket to Dublin and explained that his Uncle John would meet him in Dublin. With that he handed him the battered suitcase and gruffly said, "Good luck son." and clicked the mare to 'git up.'

Sean sat on a wooden bench in the main hall idly swinging his legs; he had already eaten the dripping and bread and hard boiled eggs packed for him by his mother. He was pleased to leave, this was his first night that he could ever remember without having the ordeal of his sister Shirley – he felt relieved.

After an hour or so, he felt apprehensive, what if John did not come for him?

Apprehensively, he got up from the wooden seat and went to the door marked gents, pushing open the door he went inside. The walls were cracked, white tiles with three wooden partitions at one side opposite a long trough with cracked porcelain sides. As he walked to the trough, the smell of stale urine heightened his agitation, almost choking him. Swallowing hard he reached the trough and hitched up his short trouser leg to pee. As he started, he felt a hand on his head. He turned sharply and looked up at the man of about 30, fat with a florid face. Hurriedly he let go of his penis and shorts, spraying urine down his leg. The fat man smiled, keeping his hand on Sean's head. Slowly but firmly the man then placed his other hand on the boys head and pushed him down towards his crutch – sticking out from his open trouser fly was an erect penis. Sean started to struggle but the fat man gripped his hair firmly with both hands and forced Sean's head down onto his penis. "Go on," he said, "suck this." Sean opened his mouth to scream but before any sound could escape the man forced his penis into the boy's mouth and moved his head backward and forward. "That's it. That's right, go on, suck it!" said the man as he began to move more vigorously.

Just then, something in Sean snapped, nobody had ever spoken to him about anything remotely like this, and he'd certainly not seen any of the farm animals do anything like this. He had known sex itself was powerful; he had already experienced several erections watching the farm animals mating; but this was different, wrong. Savagely, he bit the penis with his teeth, so violently in fact, nearly severing the head. The fat man screamed and let go of Sean's head, doubling over and screaming with shock and pain. Sean merely stood and stared down at the man with contempt. Sean now had the advantage; he was wearing hard leather farm boots with steel studs. Deliberately and carefully aimed, he kicked the man's head and watched him fall to his knees. Again and again he kicked the fat florid face until the man lay still, on his side, his damaged penis, now limp, pumped bright red blood onto the cracked concrete floor. Sean had never felt like this before, elated and flushed with excitement.

Sean opened the door and returned to the almost deserted station. As he reached the seat upon which he had placed his suitcase, a tall balding man walked up to him holding out his hand. "Sean, I'm your Uncle John, it's good to see you."

The fat man was dead before Sean had even reached his uncle's new car. That was Sean's first murder. From that day, until the time of his own execution, he was responsible for 153 people's death in total. Each one of these, he had expended with the same emotion as he had shown as he kicked the fat child molester to death: None.

CHAPTER 31

JOHN WAS A CHARTERED ACCOUNTANT, owning his own successful practice in Dublin, rich and powerful, living in an expensive detached house in the best area north of the city. Using his mother's legacy (her brains), he had on arrival in Dublin set about becoming an accountant.

Now 20 years later he was at the top. His climb to the pinnacle however, was not straight forward; he had corkscrewed his way there. Within a few months of his arrival in Dublin, he was involved with Eileen. She was the daughter of a Brigade Commander with 'The Boys' and they thought him to be a good recruit. As he gradually progressed in his chosen career he found that handling money and figures was second nature to him. 'The Boys' for the most part were not interested in the material facts. They enjoyed talking of killing and freeing all Ireland from the British bonds which enslaved their fellow countrymen in the North. Telling tales of past hero's and martyr's who died heroically at the hand of the hated British, planning raids and making bombs. There were very few members with sufficient intelligence to think beyond the tales of glory and into this vacuum stepped John McCracken. He was brilliant at placing money and shifting, buying, selling and shuffling money. What they didn't know however was as he worked the extorted pounds around, he had siphoned off hundreds of thousand of pounds for himself as he used 'The Boys' money as risk capital; putting fine profits into their bank accounts as well as his own. So good was he that he that the missing money was never discovered.

John soon recognised, that like himself, Sean had Kathleen's excellent mind. John's two children were slow and dull and John had little in common with his wife Eileen, so he took Sean to his hear and worked on his sharp mind. The accounting side did not interest Sean at all but as he grew stronger and bigger the extortion side fascinated him; power over the other people, that's what he liked. He found that secrecy, mystery and fear of the unknown gave him an edge. He deliberately created an aura to surround himself in secrecy, speaking his thoughts to nobody. People feared and hated him, mainly because of his unusual bouts of violence without any tangible reason. He encouraged the use of his Gaelic name, 'The Wolf'. This was the tongue of his mother's language, until the day he killed the fat man. To further his mystique, he formed a splinter movement called 'The Sons of Erin'. Single handedly

Sean McCracken now raised two thirds of the IRA's income through extortion, and with John overseeing this, it was doubled each year.

Sean however, had a premonition; he knew that somebody was tracking him. From what the Irishman on the mainland had told him, this man was good. Many men had died trying to outwit Sean but Sean's inner power told him that this one was different.

CHAPTER 32

ELEN DIED IN HOSPITAL, MERCIFULLY, without recovering consciousness. She had been pushed out of a moving car on the by-pass. Like the other murders, she had been violently raped, While not physically badly hurt by the assault, according to the police report, she had fractured her skull and pelvis by the fall from the car.

The police, already investigating a violent murder, and going on some information received, started the new murder enquiry by interviewing Tex. At 7:00pm on Wednesday night the two detectives assigned to the case called at 15 Stone Ring Lane. Mrs. Barber opened the door, "Yes," she enquired politely of the two men standing on the doorstep, "can I help you?"

"We would like to speak to Mr. Anderson please madam." The older of the two men said. "We are police officers." he continued, producing warrant cards.

"You'd better come in." she said. She closed the door and led them through into the lounge. This wasn't the first time Tex had been interviewed by the police, but it was the first time in his Mr. Hyde form. "Terrance!" his Aunt called from the bottom of the stairs. "There are two policemen here to see you."

"I'll be down in a moment." came back the reply.

Tex entered the lounge room door wearing a dark grey pair of slacks, blue shirt with a collar and black leather shoes on his feel.

The two detectives were momentarily taken aback. Both had been present at the hospital when Red Ted, with doctors trying to repair his damaged hand and strap his seven broken ribs, had screamed that he wanted charges for attempted murder made against Tex. This man however, looked relaxed and there was something else, an air of deliberate respectability about him. "Good evening, gentlemen," he said, "What can I do for you?"

The younger of the two detectives looked at his colleague in amazement. Looking back at Tex, he said "You've no idea why we are here?" he asked mockingly. "No idea at all?"

"None whatsoever." he replied, a smile just touching the corners of his mouth.

Recognizing a very dangerous man of undoubted intelligence, the older of the two detectives took charge of the interview from his colleague. "We are investigating the death of Helen Johnson and it is our understanding that you knew her."

"What?" exclaimed Tex, his face changing as he sat down in a chair. "When, what happened?" he asked lamely.

The two detectives again glanced at each other. "She died this morning after being sexually attacked." answered the eldest one.

"My God!" exclaimed Tex "Another one!"

"What?" said the detective.

"Well, I mean as well as that other tart that was killed."

"Tart?" enquired the detective.

"Well, that Vanessa, the Irish tart was killed a few weeks ago. That was also a sexual attack wasn't it?" he paused, recovering his pose, "Well, what can I do for you?"

"Where were you last night?" the detective enquired.

"Last night, I was in my room studying."

"All night?" asked the detective.

"Yes, all night."

"Can you prove that?" he continued.

"Oh yes," said Tex, "Auntie!" he called, "Can you come in here please?"

"Coming" was the reply from the kitchen.

She entered the room, "Can you please tell these gentlemen were I was last night?"

She looked from one to the other nervously. "You were in your room last night."

"Are you sure?" asked the detective in obvious surprise.

"Oh yes," she answered, "I took him his supper up at about 7pm, and went back at 8:30, just after my show finished, collecting his plate. Then I took him up a cup of tea at 10:30pm, when I was on my way to bed, I thought it might help him study. His light was still on at 1:30am when I got up because I couldn't sleep."

"But was he there, in his room, at that time." persisted the detective.

"Yes dear, I went in to see if he wanted anything, as I couldn't sleep I was going downstairs to warm some milk. I came back up to bed and he said goodnight to me as I passed his room."

"Thank you madam." said the detective.

"Will that be all now gentlemen?" asked Tex, rising from his chair.

Having nothing more to go on, the detectives also rose and Tex showed them to the door.

CHAPTER 33

HELEN JOHNSON LIVED WITH HER mother Mary, a staff sister at the local hospital. Mary had left her husband, Alan Johnson, when Helen was just three and set up home in a small flat in Seymour Avenue. The divorce had been amicably agreed and a regular cheque had supplemented Mary's wages until Helen was sixteen.

When Helen was ten years old, Mary's mother had died leaving her a semi-detached house in Leyland Road. Mary and Helen were very close and acted more like good friends instead of mother and daughter. To describe one was to describe the other. Slim, sensuous figures, cornflower blue eyes and fair hair, Mary's was now slightly darker. Bother were 5'4" in height.

Mary was nineteen when Helen was born and she was to be her only child. Up to the time Helen joined the Hell's Angels, she and her mother went three times a week to a local dance and exercise class together, but those days were gone. Mary did not like her daughter's fascination for motorbikes, but recognised that she had the right to do as she wanted with her life. Up to that time, their lives had been harmonious.

CHAPTER 34

ELEN JOHNSON HAD DISCOVERED AT sixteen that motorbikes excited her. When she sat astride the seat, the engines vibrations filled her whole being with a sexual desire to strong it cancelled out her normal personality. She went from her first ride on a 150cc Yamaha with sixteen year old Norman, to her last boyfriend, Johnny, on his 750cc Suzuki, who could no longer cope with her uncontrollable sexual appetite. It was then that she met Terry Anderson, who rode a 1,000cc Vincent Black Shadow. Compared to the purr of the Suzuki, the throbbing pound of the Vincent drove her wild. Tex had no problem coping with her demands; it was well within his capacity.

CHAPTER 35

NUMBER 47 KITSON AVENUE WAS a large Victorian semi-; it was a constant problem, a thorn in the side of the police and a threat to all the neighbours. About a year and a half previously, it had been placed on the market on behalf of a deceased estate for 38,000 pound.

A well spoken, well-built, muscular man of about 24 had walked into the estate agents looking for a property. Three days later, he returned and made an offer of 36,000 pound which was rejected, subsequently he raised this to 36,500 pound and it was accepted.

It was only on the completion of the sale that the next-door neighbours discovered the awful truth. The respectable, clean-cut young man who had purchased the house was in fact the leader of a chapter of Satan's disciples known as Tex; their motto was, 'do what you will'. Sometimes, on a week-end, up to 25 large chopper motorbikes roared round the large untidy garden and wild laughter and commotion caused distress and consternation to the neighbourhood. So intimidating was this band of Hell's Angels that people gave them a wide berth. The police twice raided the house, as complaints came in think and fast, but they could find nothing to charge them with apart from a warning on disturbance.

The whole chapter consisted of 30 members, who had each contributed to the deposit on the house. This gang was controlled by a five man committee consisting of Jed, Mike, Butch, Tosser and Tex; but the brains and the power were all with Tex.

Tex's real name was Terry Anderson. Five nights a week, he was a respectable, well dressed, well spoken citizen, living with his Aunt in Stone Ring Lane. Apart from his motorbike, his only other hobby was body building at the local gym.

As he usually did, on Friday night he changed into a disgusting clothing of Satan's disciple and allowed his base and vile nature full reign. He was extremely strong, and unreasonably violent, and not one of the other members dared to go against him. As he was establishing his superiority in the gang initially, he had been challenged by a man called Red Ted, known as this because of his ginger hair. Red Ted had served 3 years of a 5 year sentence in Wakefield's notorious jail for Grievous Bodily Harm. Tex had battered Red Ted unconscious in a violent fight, nailing his hand to the wooden floor with a six inch nail while he was lying on the floor of the lounge. The hospital had been unable to repair Red Ted's damaged tendons to the two middle fingers of the hand and they had to be removed. Since this incident, nobody had had the stomach for a confrontation with Tex.

CHAPTER 36

MARY JOHNSON STARED DOWN IN disbelief at the waxen face of her daughter. They had carefully masked most of the signs of violence and the post-mortem scars were hidden beneath the linen gown. She seemed screened off from it, detached and numb. The face in the wooden coffin was that of her only child, but when Helen was not there, what lay in the box was not Helen, just a Madame Tussauds wax effigy. Sadly and finally, she placed her fingertips on Helen's lips. A fat tear squeezed out from under her closed eyelids and slid down her cheek, she turned angrily and rubbed the tear away with her hand. "Don't worry Helen," she breathed to herself, "I'll pay the bastard back. I'll find out who did this to you and send him to hell."

The younger of the two detectives investigating the case was called Malcolm, Malcolm Green. He was 32, divorced and lived in a nice flat overlooking Stray Park. With his colleague, he had interviewed Mary, the day after the tragic murder. He hadn't enjoyed the interview, and he felt strongly attracted to Mary. The job had case-hardened him to sorrow, but he felt a genuine compassion for Mary. She seemed so unprepared and devastated by the news; it left such an impression on him that he called by her house a week later to check on her.

Mary was surprised by his genuine concern for her and invited him in for coffee. Malcolm sat on the settee while Mary put the kettle on, got mugs out and poured the coffee. As she came from the kitchen into the lounge she smiled up at him and he returned her smile. He's very attractive, she thought despite herself. Mary's mind jumped. This is just what she needed. Use him, he mind suddenly told her, here was lead to the bastard you are looking for. He's looking for him as well and he's professionally equipped. Mary set out to open a relationship with Malcolm, it was easier that she expected, he was already feeling a connection to her. He found Mary so attractive he was almost embarrassed to look directly at her. They chatted over the coffee.

Mary was running in top gear now, she could sense Malcolm's attraction. She took the empty mugs into the kitchen, while she was in there she splashed some Opium from her handbag that was hanging in the downstairs cloakroom. As she returned to the lounge Malcolm stood to leave. "I don't want to intrude any longer, I just felt so bad having to break the news to you last week I just had to come by and see that you were OK."

"It was nice of you to come." she replied opening her eyes wide, smiling up at him. She moved to open the front door and saw his nostrils flare as the scent of the Opium hit him. He looked at her and hesitated. Oh, go on, she thought, say what you are thinking.

"I hope you don't mind, er, mm, I mean, would you mind, could I?"

"Use the toilet?" she said sweetly.

"Yes" he said.

"Of course." she said and indicated the door beside the stairs.

"Thanks." he said as he opened the door and went in. Inside he lifted the seat and stared at himself in the mirror. Ask her you wally, he whispered to his reflection in the mirror.

He flushed the toilet and walked into the hall. Having recovered from his attack of schoolboy nervousness, he thanked her for the coffee and as he opened the front door, asked what he had meant to ask previously. "Perhaps, when you have had time to deal with this terrible business, you would like to have dinner with me?"

"Oh, that would be lovely" said Mary, "I would like that."

"Good, I'll give you a call in a few weeks then." With that, they said their goodbyes and Mary closed the door behind him.

CHAPTER 37

ONE OF HELEN'S CLOSEST FRIENDS was Janet Somerton. Mary phoned her home and asked Janet's mother to have Janet contact her. She was looking for some information about Helen's life with the Hells Angels.

Janet phone later that same night and agreed to meet Mary the next Saturday morning in Betty's Coffee House, in the High Street. Mary sat at the window table staring down the High Street. At 10:30, right on time, Janet came into the coffee house and sat at the table opposite Mary. "Hi," she said, "I don't know what to say to you, it was such a shock, I'm so sorry."

Mary sighed, "Yes." she said, and "I still cannot believe that this has happened. With an effort, Mary pulled herself back and closed down the shutter. "Janet?" she said, "I wanted to ask you about Helen's other friends, you know, the Hell's Angels people."

Janet looked embarrassed. "Well, I don't know much about them really," she said, "when Helen stared to mix with them we drifted rapidly apart. I could not stand the sight or smell of them." She shuddered. "They are revolting; I just couldn't understand what attracted her to them."

"Was Helen attached to anyone of them in particular?" she asked Janet.

"Only the leader, he's the worst, most obnoxious, animal of the whole group. The others referred to him as Tex. Before we drifted apart, and early on in her relationship with them, I invited her to a party at another friend's house; she brought this Tex with her. He's terrifying."

"In what way?" asked Mary.

"Well, he's big, and I suppose extremely good looking in a hard masculine way, but he wears the most disgusting clothes and behaves like an animal. When they arrived at the party, Helen and this Tex, Helen was quite reasonably dressed. There are other girls that live with them permanently, and they dress disgustingly like the rest of them. Leather clothes covered in studs and metal medallions, and they smell." She shuddered again at the memory.

"What happened at this party?" urged Mary.

"At first nothing, he was just quietly drinking his beer, but people at the party were sought of giving him and Helen a wide berth. Then about 11 o'clock, there was a commotion in the front garden. Another 8 or 9 of these Hell's Angels Disciples had turned up. Honestly, the garden at the front of the house was super, all flower beds and beautiful lawns. They rode round and round, shouting and swearing, blowing loud horns and klaxons. If that wasn't enough, they started throwing beer cans through the windows of the house. This Tex went out into the garden and brought them all into the house. Somebody phoned the police. There was pandemonium, girls shrieking and crying, these Hells Disciples people just wrecked the house completely. Then, as quickly as it had all started, they all disappeared, just before the police arrived. Tex had stayed, as if nothing had happened. It was strange, like he had everyone mesmerized, even the police found it difficult to pin him to the disturbance. He hadn't actually been directly involved, but he seemed to have orchestrated the whole incident without being involved at all. Each time I saw him after that, and that was only 2 or 3 times, I found him disturbing and unsettling. He is the most evil person I have ever encountered." As she spoke these words, Mary saw the hairs on her arms rise as she shuddered again as she recalled.

Mary looked down at her cream cake and coffee. The coffee was cold and the cake untouched, Janet's too. They had been so engrossed, they had forgotten them.

Mary gave her meeting with Janet a great deal of thought, could this Tex have murdered Helen? Surely not! He wouldn't have had to rape her to get sex; she had given it to him. The telephone brought her thoughts rapidly to an end. "Hello," a pleasant voice said. "It's Malcolm."

As they came out of the theatre, this had been their second date together, Malcolm asked Mary back to his flat for a night cap. Once inside, she gave him her coat and settled on the rug in front of the gas fire while he poured out a whisky and a martini. He then joined her on the rug. He placed both the glasses on the stone hearth, taking her hands in his and he looked into her eyes from only a few inches away.

"You know, he said, "I'm getting very, very fond of you." Mary smiled and leaned into him, kissing him full on the lips, a long kiss. With the tip of her tongue, she traced the outline of his bottom lip. The tip of his tongue joined hers; she came away from him slowly, letting their lips stick for an instant. She breathed through her mouth and he inhaled, they both breathed each other's essence. It had been over two years since her pulses had raced like this. It happened too quickly for her to control it, she had only meant to use him, now it was different. Slowly, they rose, still holding hands. She kicked off her shoes as he placed his hands behind her back. Slowly he drew down the zip, taking the shoulders off, the dress fell to the floor. As if in a dream, she undid the buttons of his shirt, one at a time, then his trouser belt. His breathing was ragged. Placing his head slightly to one side, he kissed her right ear gently, and then behind, then below, his tongue traced a path on to the shoulder. Gently, he undid her bra; her breasts fell free, taking one strap off, then the other. Her breasts were firm and the nipples stood straight out, hard and puckered as if she were cold. Slowly his hands travelled down her back to the swell of her bottom, sliding under her panties, he pushed them down. She undid his grousers gently, pulling down the zip. Slowly, together, they bent at the knees and sagged onto the fluffy rug. She took hold of her panties and one leg at a time took them off. His trousers followed her panties onto the settee.

After dancing classes, Mary often had a sun bed session, and her body was a lovely delicate golden-brown all over. In contrast,

Malcolm's body was white, his long muscular legs covered in coarse black hair. In the light of the lamp on the coffee table he could see her complete body, round feminine curves, the triangle of gingery-blonde hairs, thick and luxuriant disappearing between the apex of her legs. By this time, his underpants had distorted completely by the violent mushroom growth from beneath. She pulled them off and gasped as she saw his manhood. Slowly, their bodies came together, locked in spontaneous passion. To and fro they rocked and writhed, until slowly a rhythm began to emerge from the chaos. Together they formed their harmonies, which carried them onto a flood tide, a peak; they became rigid and clung together in climax.

Slowly Malcolm raised himself to his knees and they came apart, wetly and reluctantly. Mary clung to him, not wanting to lose the moment. He flopped over onto his back and lay beside her, touching hands.

"Oh Malcolm!" she cried and started sobbing. "Oh Malcolm," she said again between sobs, "that was, that was…." she sought for words. He placed a finger on her lips and cuddled her. She snuggled up into his shoulder and he hugged her tightly. The Durex slid, unnoticed, from him and fell onto the fluffy rug. As Mary turned to press her body closer to him, she felt the cold clingy latex on her bottom. "Ugh!' she cried, holding the spent condom up like a discarded, deflated children's balloon. They both collapsed into peals of passionate, relieved laughter.

"I don't even remember putting it on, let alone taking it off." he said difficulty between fits of laughter.

CHAPTER 38

Mary's shoes hurt and her calves ached from standing all day. She had been on duty since 6:30am and she was tired. Dr. Melton had had a full day, starting at 10:00am, with only a ¾ hour break; another hour and Mary could go home. The next patient was T. Anderson, problems with his right hand. Mary went into the waiting room, "Mr. Anderson." she called, and the man stood up and walked towards her. He was dressed in brown trousers, tightly cut and of good quality. Expensive leather casual shoes, a cream shirt with a dark brown tie and an expensive designer leather jacket completed his outfit. He smiled as he approached. He had strong white teeth set behind evenly behind full lips, a bluish colour to his chin and cheeks showed a strong beard though he was clean shaven. His light brown eyes met hers and his smile broadened. A shudder ran through Mary involuntarily as she caught the full power of the man. He was over six foot and beneath his shirt, she could see his powerful chest muscles through the thin material. The trousers were tightly fitted and his legs, though not excessive, were powerful. One hand was bandaged with crepe bandages, the other was large but clean with well manicured nails. Mary pulled herself together with a conscious will. "Follow me please." and she turned and walked swiftly to the doctors room. The man followed close behind her.

"Mr. Anderson," the doctor looked up from his desk, "sit down, please." He removed the bandages to reveal a red and swollen hand. "What happened here?" he enquired.

"I trapped it in the car door." he said easily".

Dr Melton examined the hand and moved the fingers. Although the man appeared not to react, Mary saw the muscles at the jaw line bunch and his biceps twitched as he caught the pain from the movement. "This is a mess." the doctor said, also noticing the man's almost unperceivable reaction. "Do you want a local anesthetic while I examine your hand?"

"No," the man replied, "just do what you have to."

"There's a rather bad wound between your first and second knuckle which looks infected. Also there is some restriction to movement of your knuckle joint, almost as if you have something stuck in there. I really think I must anaesthetize it before I can properly examine you."

"OK, whatever you must do." the man said.

Five minutes after the injection, the hand was completely numb. The doctor carefully probed the wound. "There is something in there." he said. Taking a pair of forceps, he carefully probed inside the knuckle joint. "Ah, here we are." He dropped the small fragment into a stainless steel bowl on the table to inspect it better. He looked from the white fragment directly into the man's eyes. The man met his stare nonchalantly. The doctor opened his mouth to comment, but looking into the light brown eyes, which were still holding his, he thought better of it. He disinfected the wound, put two small stitches in it and covered it with a surgical dressing. "That should heal quickly." he said. "Just have your GP remove the stitches in a few days time."

"Thanks Doc." With that, he stood, nodded to the doctor, smiled at Mary and walked out.

The doctor stood very still at the table, staring after the man for a while. Mary looked at the fragment in the bowl. It was a human tooth, snapped off at gum level.

CHAPTER 39

ON SATURDAY AFTERNOON, MARY WALKED across the market place with her shopping. Her car was parked behind Peterson's store. She hear a continuous roar of several motorbikes coming from Town Hill, into the square poured a dozen or so motorbikes ridden by the most terrifying looking people imaginable. Hell's Angels of the worst possible type. As Mary watched, they rode around the square twice, slowly, and then all together stopped in the car park. Two or three had shaven heads, others had long straggled unkempt hair. All wore tattered leather jackets with the sleeves cut out, exposing tattooed arms, jeans with holes and ragged patches on the back of the jackets. A skull with the words, apparently embroidered on, read 'Satan's Disciples'. Boots with studs on the soles finished off the uniforms; several had girls on their pillions.

As they removed their assorted crash helmets and German military helmets Mary's breath caught in her throat. "My God," she breathed to herself, "that's Anderson." The realization was like a slap in the face "Tex, the leader." Janet Somerton's words came flooding back to her, "He's terrifying." On his pillion was a very pretty young girl of about seventeen. Mary watched, Tex smacked her on the behind through her tight leather jeans, but so hard and violent that the girl winced and cringed, gently rubbing herself where he had struck her.

They walked across to the chuck wagon, a hot dog and hamburger van. An old woman, with a bag and a terrier on a lead, walked along the pavement in front of the van. As Tex stepped onto the pavement, he tripped over the little dog, which yelped. Looking down, Tex kicked the dog against the walk, it collapsed in a heap. The old lady knelt down beside it and cradled its head. Mary raced over to aid the old lady. The disciples ignored them both and gathered around the chuck wagon. Mary looked at the little dog; it was in a bad way. "Danny, Danny." the old lady was quietly sobbing. Mary put her arm around her, "Come on," she said, "we'll take him to the vet." She scooped up the little dog and shepherded the old lady to her car. Mary paused before getting into the car and looked at Tex; he looked directly back at her and smiled, holding up his bandaged hand.

The vet said the dog had bad internal injuries and advised them to have the dog put to sleep. The old lady started to cry, "Can't you save him?" asked Mary.

"I could try," said the vet, "but it will be expensive."

Mary looked at the old lady's worn cheap coat and scuffed shoes, tears were streaming down her seamed wrinkled cheeks. "OK," said Mary, "do what you can. I'll pay the bill."

The vet smiled. "I'll do my best, I promise." He then winked at Mary and added, "Without breaking the bank."

Mary took the old lady to the council flat she called home, and made her a cup of tea; she felt truly sorry for the woman. "I'm sure the vet will be able to save him." she said, trying to reassure her.

"You are very kind. I'm so grateful to you." she hesitated; "They didn't have to hurt him." she said and started to weep again. Mary put her arm around the old woman to calm her down. She looked around the flat, it smelt old and sour and made Mary feel depressed. "Will you be alright now?" she asked.

"Yes, thank you dear, I'll be fine."

Mary had an overwhelming need to get out into the fresh air. At home she ran a bath; the afternoon had left her with a feeling of inadequacy. She was fully aware of Tex's powerful presence. She had seen Dr Jeckle and Mr. Hyde. She like neither and greatly feared both. She lay in the hot scented water and let her mind wander. Her thoughts went to Helen, lying in the morgue; Tex's smiling face became that of the devil himself. Suddenly she was overcome by nausea. Quickly she got out of the bath and was violently sick into the toilet.

CHAPTER 40

MARY SAT ON THE SETTEE, her legs folded up underneath her. How could she confirm what she already was convinced of: That Tex had killed Helen in a fit of his obvious violent and dangerous schizophrenic nature? Although she was not happy with the thought, Malcolm was the obvious answer. He was now very much attached to her and she, in spite of herself, was beginning to admit strong emotions for him. The problem was how to get what she wanted from him without destroying what they had started to build. She made up her mind to gently probe him to find how the investigations were progressing at the next opportunity.

Malcolm phoned her the very next day and they arranged to go out; he would pick her up at 7:00pm from her house.

At 5:30 Mary ran a bath and poured nearly a whole bottle of bath essence into the water. The powerful perfume filled the whole house. Gingerly she tested the hot water and slowly emerged into its foamy depths. Stretching in its warmth, goose pimples formed on the parts of her body not under the water. A shiver ran down her spine, she loved hot soapy baths; they gave her a sensual luxuriant feel. As she lay there, half asleep, she became aware of the telephone ringing downstairs. She rose from the foam filled bath and grabbed a large towel, which she wrapped around her.

Just as she reached the phone, it stopped ringing. Standing in the lounge, dripping water onto the carpet, she waited for it to ring again.

After about 30 seconds of nothing, she removed the receiver from the instrument and set it on the table, returning upstairs to her bath.

It was 6:55pm as she settled into an arm chair with a glass of wine and replaced the receiver. Almost immediately the phone started shrilling. Before she could speak, "Hello, hello," came an agitated voice from the receiver.

"Malcolm?" she quizzed.

"Helen, I've been trying for hours to phone you but the line has been engaged."

Feeling a little guilty, Helen said "Yes, I'm sorry, but I've had a lot of trouble with it just lately. You're supposed to be picking me up about now, where are you?"

"That's why I've been trying to contact you. I'm afraid that I will be late. I won't be able to make it until 9:30pm. Sorry Helen, it's my job." Malcolm apologised.

"That's OK." she said "Not to worry; I will see you when you get here. Damn, she thought, as she poured herself another glass of wine.

Malcolm arrived at 10:15, he was shattered. By this time Helen had finished the bottle of wine and had been prepared to be totally awful to him, until she saw Malcolm's state and her hear melted. He flopped onto the settee. She was standing with her back to the fire, hands on hips, observing him, "You look dreadful," she said.

"If I look as bad as I feel, then I'm not surprised." was his comment.

"Have you eaten?"

"No."

"Hungry?"

"Starving!"

"Okay, don't move." said Mary. She placed a large whiskey in his hand, the ice tingled against the glass, and he smiled up at her. She kissed him on the forehead; he placed his hand behind her neck and pulled her head down to kiss her on the lips. Gently pulling away, Helen went into the kitchen. He heard the microwave ping as he stared into the fire and then closed his eyes.

Waking to the sound of milk bottles, he sat with a start. A large blue blanket slipped off him and fell to the carpet. He looked at his watch, 5:30am. My God, he had slept all night, the last thing he remembered was looking into the fire. He yawned and stretched, his jacket was neatly folded over the chair back and his brown shoes on the floor beside the chair. The glass of whiskey was sitting on the coffee table, the ice long since melted. He stood and went into the kitchen and filled the kettle, then went to the bathroom.

Carefully, he carried the two mugs into the bedroom, placing them quietly on the bedside table. He gently lifted the sheet and slid into the bed beside her, wrapping her in a warm embrace.

"Well, you look and smell better than you did last night." Mary told him as they sat up to drink their coffee a little while later.

He smiled at her affectionately, "Early morning sex always improves the quality of life, don't you think?"

Mary laughed and hit him with a pillow, "You cheeky sod, you practically helped yourself while my back was turned."

The euphoric mood Mary felt, began to slip away as she put her mid to her quest for revenge on Helen's killer. "What made you so late last night?' she asked Malcolm. He looked at her for a long while without answering. Up to now he had never discussed his work with her, now he felt the need to talk, he trusted her.

"Are you sure you want to know?" he asked eventually. Now it was Mary's turn to look, without speaking, being sure to choose her words carefully.

She lay back on the pillows, "I would like to be part of your life." she finally said.

"I know that nothing will bring Helen back, such a young, happy girl, it is tragic. That kind of thought can become corrosive and eat away your insides. I need to talk about it, to be involved. Perhaps you could discuss with me how the investigation is going; perhaps I could even be of help in some way?"

"OK," said Malcolm, "I understand and appreciate your wanting to help and up to now, I have not been sure of your reaction to Helen's murder. Let me explain: In most murders of this horrific type, the people left behind, the close relatives go through stages grief. First shock and horror, sadness for someone close suddenly cut off, gone forever. This is usually followed by a deep hatred and an urge for revenge."

Although Mary did not show it, Malcolm had just described her exact feelings. She must try to persuade him that her desire for revenge could be satisfied by helping the police bring the murderer to justice. My god, she thought to herself, to think of this bastard being sentenced to life. Life indeed, what a laugh, 12 years more like and not even that in certain circumstances. No, this one was an eye for an eye. Helen would not return after 12 years and she was blameless so neither would this one, this one was for good.

Malcolm interrupted her thoughts by saying what Mary had thought from the day she saw Tex at the doctors surgery, "We have strong suspicions that terry Anderson in responsible. He has definite psychopathic traits and Helen was known to be (choosing his words) associated with him and his friends. We have had him in for questioning on several occasions; he is a very shrewd and devious man, highly dangerous and unstable. Unfortunately, he has an unshakeable alibi."

"How can an alibi from any of that scum be reliable?" Mary blurted out before she could stop herself.

Malcolm turned to look at her, slightly surprised at her tone, "Oh no, not from the Devil's Disciples." he said "This was from his Aunt – a very respectable woman indeed – she confirms he was in his room the whole night that Helen was killed."

Mary's mind flashed back to the Mr. Anderson at the surgery.

CHAPTER 41

Boom! With a loud crack, the sawn-off shotgun jerked in his hand, the 12SG lead balls smashing into the ragged denim clad knee shattering the bone and driving the dirty material into the tattered flesh. The Chopper bike slid from beneath the Hells Angel and the coke bottle full of petrol he was holding, with the already burning cloth fuse, dropped to the concrete drive. Instantly a pool of flame engulfed the motor bike and rider – Tex grinned and a psychopathic fury tugged at his powerful features.

A full blown war had erupted at 47 Kitson Avenue between the 'Devil's Disciples' and the 'Death's Head hells' Angels' from the nearby town of Dardfield. The heavy metal music of New Dawn had drowned out the first onslaught of a brick being thrown through the front window. Then there was the unmistakable sound of five choppers roaring up the drive. Tex had shot the nearest to the house, two more had been engulfed in the flames from the Molotov cocktail held by the now badly burnt first bikie.

Red Ted had rushed out from the back garden flailing a bicycle chain, bringing another bikie to the ground. A further 3 came rushing up the driveway, having left their machines on the roadside. A huge bearded giant swung a baseball bat and hit Tex across his ear, fracturing his skull. Falling to the ground, he dropped the shotgun and second barrel had discharged 2 ½ oz of lead into directly into Red Ted's back, shattering his spine just below his pelvis. Another

Molotov cocktail sailed through the shattered window and exploded into fames in the front room.

From across the street, two residents frantically dialed 999 police, fire & ambulance. The fire engines were the first to arrive, by this time the house was well alight. Within minutes the police arrived; there were 4 of the 'Devils Disciple's' left in the front garden; Red Ted was out the back, completely paralyzed from the waist down; Tex was unconscious with a fractured skull; Frank Stewart was dead from multiple stab wounds and Arthur Danbury was sitting with his back against the side wall with a broken arm and third degree burns from his left shoulder to his knee and suffering from severe shock.

Of the rival gang there was; one with badly damaged knee and severe burns, barely alive; one dead from a broken neck; and a third badly burned but alive. They were taken by ambulance, with a police escort, to the local hospital.

CHAPTER 42

MARY PUSHED HER HAIR BACK and stretched, it had been a hard day; on top of her own shift, she was covering for a sick sister in casualty. The emergency bell started to ring and the first of the ambulances arrived carrying the wounded but still alive casualties. The first was Red Ted; he was screaming abuse at the ambulance men, Dr Castle took a quick look at him, "4cc of Nembutal, staff please." he said. As the drug flowed into his system, Ted quieted his body relaxing despite his aggression until his held fell to one side. As they turned him over the dreadful wound became obvious, "My god." said Dr Castle as he carefully started to remove the tattered leather jacket, "What a mess."

Over his shoulder, Mary saw the next stretcher being carried in, temporary bandages covering his face but she could still see that it was Terry Anderson. A strange elation spread through her, perhaps he was dead. Then another emotion shook her, as she grappled with it, she was shocked to realize that she hoped he was alive so that she was still able to wreak her own revenge on him herself. The primitive thought shocked her, yet gave her a pleasant sensation. Putting the thought aside, she returned to assist Dr Castle, "Go and check on the other one, staff." he told her. She turned again and looked down at the object of her hate, he was unshaven and wearing a filthy leather jacket with disgusting obscene badges sewn on it. His denim jeans had holes in them exposing black coarse hairs on his legs, a huge black Swastika hung around his neck. She looked at the strong powerful jaw and large nose; another unhealthy indescribable shudder ran through her body; he was the very embodiment of evil, she forced the animal waves which radiated from him away. Gently she probed his head beneath the bandages, even in deep unconsciousness he groaned, she felt the soft mushy depression behind his left ear, the blood soaked slowly through the heavy bandage.

Malcolm winked at Mary as he came in, she smiled a tired smile, and neither spoke to the other. "Can you give me a statement Dr." he said, "what do you think happened?"

"Oh I don't pretend to know what happened Sergeant, but I can tell you the status of the victims or participants. What happened will be up to you to extract from them!" He picked up several report form cards.

"Ted Smith," he began, *"male aged about 25 with damage to right hand, 2 fingers missing – severe damage to base of spine, shot gun wound at close range causing complete paralysis from the neck down – he is stable at present."*

"Terrance Anderson – male aged 26-27 – fractured skull, still unconscious with no apparent brain damage evident from preliminary brain scans – further tests to be carried out."

"One, still unnamed male aged 18-19 dead, several deep stab wounds, one penetrating liver and cutting main arterial causing internal hemorrhage."

"Arthur Danbury – aged 18 – fractured left tibia, 3rd degree burns to left side – condition stable but patient is in severe shock."

"Another unnamed man aged 22-23 – badly damaged right knee, lower left amputated – severe burns to 90% of his body – not expected to survive the next 24 hours."

"One male aged 25-30 – 50% 3rd degree burns to entire body – in severe shock but considered stable."

Dr Castle looked up at the sergeant, "The look as though they have been in the Vietnam war. From the clothes they were wearing, they have been, or are members of, 'Hell's Angels Club'. I don't think you will get much out of any of them for a few days."

"Thanks Dr." Malcolm moved to speak to the uniformed officer, "Could you please see that they stay under police guard until I can interview them."

"Right away." he replied.

Mary set about her plan. She called regularly into Arthur Danbury's room, without his Hells' Angels uniform he was just a young boy, his short cropped hair had given him a college boy look, now dressed in hospital pyjamas he looked much like any other 18 year old lad. He was heavily sedated, no-one had been to visit him since he was admitted and he had told the doctor that he had no next of kin. Mary took full advantage of his state of shock. He was drowsy and pleasantly full of pain killers when Mary came off duty and went into his room. The police had placed each of the members in private wards until the investigations were completed. Still wearing her nurse uniform, the constable had not even looked at her. She had only been in the room a few minutes when the constable changed shift. The new constable didn't even know she was in there. She sat on the bed and took his hand in hers. "How are you feeling?" she said softly.

The boy smiled up at her, "OK." he said.

"Good" she said, patting his hand. "Now, where do you live?"

"The Chapter House."

"No, where is your home?" she persisted.

"I ran away from Borstal."

Slowly and gently she continued talking to him, gaining his confidence. Caused by a mixture of his drugged state and his immaturity, he yearned for a mother figure and Mary filled the bill nicely. "Tell me about Tex." she said carefully. Fear flitted across his eyes and he turned his head toward the window, slowly he turned back and she could see tears forming in the corner of his eyes. He closed his eyes and two tears ran off his cheeks onto the pillow. She placed a hand on his forehead. Now in complete control, she stifled her natural compassion and probed deeper. "Tell me about him." she gently asked again.

"He's evil." he whispered. "He does terrible things to people."

"What sort of things."

He turned his head again and was quiet for a while. Without looking at Mary he said, "I hate him, I wish he was dead. He beat his Aunty senseless and knocked out one of her teeth."

"Why would he do such a thing?" Mary asked.

"For fun I suppose." he replied, still looking out the window.

Mary thought for a while, remembering back to the tooth in Tex's hand. On instinct, without really thinking, Mary went on to ask "Does he have any weaknesses, anything at all that he is frightened of?"

"Suppose he did, I couldn't tell you, if he found out he would kill me?" he said in the softest voice.

Mary smiled, "Who's going to tell him? Not me, and if you don't, nobody will know will they?"

The drugs had relaxed him more than he realized, lowering his caution, and Mary's soothing presence gave him a wish to confide in somebody. Who knows, it might even take away some of the burden and make him feel some importance. He knew the 'Great Tex' had an Achilles heel and the knowledge had given him a certain secret power. Now that everything had combined to produce an atmosphere of complete trust and euphoria, he was prepared to share this secret that he had been carrying for some six months' an insurance policy had had discovered by accident.

CHAPTER 43

THE 747 LANDED AT TRIPOLI airport. Clyde joined the queue at 'other passports'. "Why are you coming to Libya?" the official demanded looking up from Clyde's 'special' passport'.

"To collect tender documents and discuss details of the new hospital at Mizratah."

"How long will you be here?"

"Oh, just a few days!" Clyde replied.

The official thumbed through the passport until he reached the visa stamped by the Peoples Bureau in Dublin. He stared for sometime at the stamp as this was unusual, but he realized that it may not be wise to comment and stamped the passport. The man looked hard at Clyde, "Have you anything to declare?" he asked. "No" said Clyde. With that, the official threw the passport across the desk. Clyde stopped it with his hand before it reached the edge. Clyde picked up his overnight bag and walked over to the Avis rent-a-car kiosk.

"Clyde Machin" he stated to the Arab behind the count "you have a car for me?" The man smiled and picked up the phone. He dialled a number and a few seconds later he said into the mouthpiece, "The Infidel has arrived." He turned back to Clyde, "Your transport is waiting outside the entrance effendi. Clyde walked out of the airport.

The air was hot and moist and smelt of a mixture of camels and cheap cigarettes. A small yellow fiat came around the corner on two wheels screeching to a halt beside Clyde. The door flung open and Clyde bent down to look at the driver, who was a young Arab. He had a long aristocratic face with a large hooked nose. He looked at Clyde and his face cracked into a large grin, showing big white teeth, his dark eyes sparkled with excitement. Get in Infidel, before the police decide to investigate you. Clyde threw his bag on the back seat and climbed in beside the driver, who was wearing a white T shirt and faded blue jeans. On the front of the T shirt was a circle with a diagonal line running through it. The line went from one side of the circle and cut the other side, from the end of the line outside the circle 3 drops fell onto the letter M. The young Arabs hair was jet black and long it was gathered into a pony tail and tied with a blue and white piece of material.

As they sped off through the busy streets Clyde looked quizzically at him. The youth looked back and smiled. "You are wondering who I am?" he asked in a cultured English accent. "I am Prince Assam Al-i Akram Jalude, son of Mamood al-i–Akram, who was executed by the secret police for his part in the attempted over throw of the monkey you eats camel dung.

Clyde laughed "By that exalted title I presume you mean Colonel Gaddafi?"

He is no more a Colonel than the lead camel that walks first in the caravan. He has ruined this country with his obsession with weapons; there are more weapons here than there are men to use them. What good are sophisticated weapons in the hands of men used to throwing stones? His tribe are tenders of goats in the Al-Kyrah valley throwing stones at the lion." The little Fiat almost knocked a fat elderly Arab off his bicycle. The prince blew the horn loudly "Get out of the way goat herd" he shouted.

A phone rang, startling Clyde, and then he noticed a car phone under the dash board. The prince picked up the hand set and spoke into it in Arabic and replaced the phone. "He has gone to the house of Hassan Gamall the man you came with on the big silver bird." "My friends call me Assam" the prince said.

"Pleased to meet you Assam" Clyde said holding out his hand which the prince shook warmly as he pulled to the side of the road. They had stopped opposite a large indoor market.

"Wait here Infidel, I won't be long." He ran across into the market and returned a few minutes later with a girl about the same age as himself. She had long dark hair, delicate high cheekbones and huge dark eyes framed by long eye lashes. "This is Princess Adele Ali Akram Jalood, known to her friends as Ally. She will be your guide and contact. I will see you tonight." and with that he vanished back into the market.

"Hi" said the girl and climbed into the drivers' seat. "You are booked into the Tripoli Hilton. Assam calls you the Infidel, but I cannot call you that, what is your name?"

"Clyde" he said feeling very awkward and slightly tongue tied.

As they drove through the city, he searched for something to say to start a conversation, while studying her from the corner of his eye. Army life and his career had kept him away from female company, but now he desperately wanted to get closer to this beautiful girl that had been thrust upon him.

She pulled up at the entrance of the Hilton Hotel. The foyer was very impressive; huge sprays of vibrant coloured bougainvillea, red and purple, emblazoned the entrance. Water cascaded into pools in which swam giant Japanese carp, called Coy, lazily swimming between white and pink lilies.

"You book in and I will see you in the coffee lounge in one hour" said Ally.

Clyde booked in and the porter carried his leather bag up to room 568. He stripped off quickly and showered in the marble bathroom. He shaved using the sterilized razor provided by the hotel and generously splashed on the eve san Laurent after shave from the courtesy pack provided.

The coffee shop was packed as Clyde waked self consciously into the room. And although his tight jeans and cutaway T-shirt showed his good physique, he felt white and pale compared with the dark skinned people lounging in the chairs and standing at the tables. Ally stood up and waved, she was at a table near the garden overlooking the pool. Two other men were seated with her. Clyde felt slightly irritated by this as he had wanted to speak to her on her own. He walked over and sat on the chair she pulled out for him. "These are two more soldiers of the desert" she said in a low voice "Chalhede and Achmed." The two men smiled and bowed heads slightly. "This is Clyde 'the Infidel'" she said in a low soft voice. They smiled again.

Chalhede leant forward towards Clyde "I believe you use the bow" he said.

Clyde was surprised by this "Yes I can use a bow but I didn't bring" one he said.

"No matter." said Chalhede "I too am a bowman, perhaps we will get the chance to shoot together while you are here."

"Yes" said Clyde.

Just then the other man leaned forward "I believe you kill with out weapons, just your bare hands" he grinned.

Clyde started back in his chair "What is this he said?"

Ally leaned towards him; he could smell Jasmine as she moved. "Humour him" she said "all his family were killed by the secret police when he was young. They tortured, raped and then killed his mother in front of him. He has been avenging her ever since. He has killed dozens." She reached out and took Achmeds hand pulling it towards her, turning it over, for Clyde to see. She pushed up his shirt sleeve to reveal a line of thin scars running the length of his arm, starting at his wrist and ending at his inner elbow. In total there were about 40 small scars. "Each scar represents a member of the Secret Police sent to speak to Allah" she said softly.

Not sure what to say, Clyde looked at the man, who in turned stared back at him. Suddenly he grinned at Clyde, revealing a missing tooth. The grin was so infectious that Clyde broke into a smile and shook his hand vigorously. "Yes, like you, I have killed with my bare hands.

"Leave us now" Ally said to the two men.

Clyde felt goose bumps, he shivered, and the hairs on the back of his neck stood up as he looked at Ally, the hotel was International so women were not expected to stick to strict Muslim dress. She had on a simple white cotton shift and tight Levi jeans. She had small pert breasts, and without a bra, her nipples stood out against the thin material. Through the gap between the buttons he could see the swell of her breasts. Slowly, he raised his eyes to meet hers; she acknowledged his attention and smiled. She liked this quiet Infidel!

"I am completely in the dark" he said "I was told in Ireland that I would be contacted by someone in Tripoli by going to the avis counter and giving them my name. And now I find myself here."

She laid a delicate hand on his arm. The long slim fingers felt cool on his skin. The nails were long and elegant. "First tell me why you are here?"

"I came following the trail of an Irish Terrorist called Sean McCracken. He, in turn, is here in Tripoli to meet several terrorist organisations to organise funds to finance terrorism throughout the world. I have personal issues with this man and I intend to kill him." Clyde had no reservations in telling Ally this, after all, only a few hours in her company and he felt he could tell her anything.

"I see." she said. "We are Libyan Aristocracy; our ancestors ruled the desert valley between The Gulf of Sidra and Egypt, a territory twice the size of England. When Gaddafi rose to power, the predominately Damagni tribesmen, traditionally Bedouin nomads, supported him and an Islamic state was declared. All hereditary titles were disbanded and a commissar, appointed by the peoples committee, was sent to each of the 8 regions to report on the communications of the kingdoms. In order to try and suppress any form of rising up of traditional type of ruling by the 8 royal families, an important member of each was made a general in the state army. Two years ago, four of these got together and plotted the overthrow of Gaddafi. Somehow, information got to the secret police and the four were arrested, along with hundreds of the influential members of the 8 ruling families. My father, Manhram Ali Akram Jalude, was executed by the secret police along with two of the others."

"What happened to the fourth?" asked Clyde.

"It was discovered that he had betrayed my father and the other two in exchange for his freedom and a great deal of money. As he journeyed north with his new found fortune, he met with an accident, becoming a thin scar on Ahmed's arm. This country is rich in oil and other minerals but it is being raped by the communist committees and the people placed in charge by Gaddafi's policies. Freedom is a thing of the past, there is no democracy, we are in danger over here of being overheard and reported to the secret police. We run an underground anti-state movement, at the present it is small and uncoordinated but getting stronger each day. We are helped by several countries but not openly of course. In fact, we are not known or recognised by anywhere yet.

"I was sent to London, along with Ashan, to study; him mechanical and engineering and me English and economics. While we were there we were contacted by British Intelligence, eager to have a pipeline into Libya with problems with the dreadful shooting of the policewoman. Incidentally, the official who carried out the shooting was welcomed by the ruling committee as a hero when he returned to Tripoli after being expelled. Three weeks later as he walked out of a restaurant with a prostitute, Cahlede put a shaft through the centre of his chest from 85 paces; he was dead before he hit the pavement. We have worked on several occasions with your people, also being targeted for the American raid on Tripoli recently. As I say, at present we are no more than a nuisance to the central committee, but we are growing. One day we will oust this stupid, brainless system and replace it with democracy before, I hope, the oil runs out."

"How did you know about me?" Clyde asked.

"The British Intelligence has a small office on the wharf operating as a washing machine spares importing company, one of their men, Jack Castleford, runs it as a genuine business. It actually makes a lot of money. Ashan is the delivery man for the company, and because all commerce must run with Libyan control, he is Managing Director. Employees of British Intelligence are not allowed to make money, therefore Jack is paid direct into his bank in England so the profits are ours, good hey!" she grinned.

"Come, I will take you on a tour of our city." she said as she stood. Clyde rose with her, but hesitated when she suddenly placed her hand on his arm. Two men had entered the room, each wearing the standard brown T-shirt of the peoples of the Militia, brown fatigue pants tucked in calf length boots. As they walked into the bar and started talking to the man behind the counter, Adel took Clyde's arm and led him quickly out over the terrace into the pool area not stopping until they were shielded by thick bushes.

"How did you know they were after you?" Clyde questioned, genuinely concerned. Clyde had never been in love. Never even felt anything much about a girl before. Now, as he looked at this Arab princess, he realised he had strong feelings for her and it unnerved him. "Tell me," he said as they climbed into the yellow fiat in the hotel car park. "What does the motive mean on Ashan's T-shirt?"

Adel broke into peals of laughter, "My, you are observant." she said when she had recovered. "The circle is the traditional symbol of the desert warriors; all round watchful and alert as the eagle which can see behind as well as in front. The diagonal line represents the sword; a cutting edge across the desert. And the three drops are the desert warrior peeing on the Muramor, the monkey who eats camel dung."

She drove like her brother, in fact, everybody in Tripoli seemed to drive the same way; erratic, frantic and without regard for other people. They were weaving in and out of the narrow streets, the little squeaky horn constantly blowing, peep peep.

"Let's look at this Hassan Gahamahl's palace." Clyde said, "Whereabouts is it?"

"It's out on the other side of town, we'll go there now." she said as the phone started to ring. She picked up the receiver and spoke rapidly in Arabic then passed the phone to Clyde, "Assam to speak to you." she said.

Clyde took the receiver. "Infidel," he listened "how are you getting on with the princess?"

He could feel the flush spread up his neck from under his shirt. He looked at her profile, "OK." he said in a noncommittal voice, "She's OK."

"The man you seek to follow has left the house of Hassam Gahamahl; he has gone to a meeting with several other people at the People's conference centre."

"Can you identify the other people there?" asked Clyde.

"Most of them, yes. I will try and get details of all of them for you Infidel; can you now put Adel back on?"

Clyde passed the phone back to Adel who smiled as she took it from him. As she listened to her brother she looked across at Clyde and smiled again. She then spoke Arabic to her brother and replaced the handset beneath the dashboard.

"We are to meet him tonight at our house at 7:00pm when he will have more information of the meeting. He tells me that I must be careful; Cahlede has told him that you look upon me with a great hidden depth but I told him to mind his own business." She turned to Clyde, "So, do you look upon me with great hidden depth oh visitor from the island of past glories?"

Clyde found it difficult to answer her, so great were his emotions. In all his life he had never experienced this turbulence; he had always remained cool and detached. Even when Vanessa was murdered, his detachment had been complete. Now, he was like a little schoolboy, he could feel the colour spreading up past his ears and he had no way of controlling it. Before he was forced into an even more embarrassing position he was saved by a sudden commotion on the road in front of them. A lorry, piled high with wire baskets filled with live chickens, had collided with a donkey and cart loaded with vegetables. The road was amassed with chickens, cabbages, tomatoes and people shouting and arguing. The little fiat screeched to a halt amidst the confusion. Clyde looked at the mayhem and put his hand on the door handle to open it. "No." said Adel, "Wait."

It was only a matter of seconds before they heard the wail of a siren closing in and a military jeep skidded to a stop; 4 men leapt out wearing brown T-shirts and carrying AK47 assault rifles. Without any delay, they started firing the weapons in the air. The driver of the donkey and cart was a fat Arab with a long dirty white Shaba and a grey turban, the leader of the men rushed up and hit him hard in the middle with the butt of his rifle, sending him to the ground. Seeing this, the driver of the truck, a man of about 25, leapt into his cab and started the engine; revving the motor he lurched forward, skidding and bumping over the cages of chickens and vegetables. Another of the 4 men fired a burst of gunfire at the departing truck as it rapidly disappeared around a corner. The driver of the jeep and the man beside him remained impassively seated throughout these events.

Now the passenger emerged from the jeep, adjusted his peak cap, and strode to the centre of road and started directing traffic while his men kicked the wire cages and vegetables off the road.

Clyde and Adel, still in the fiat, were behind a large white Toyota which was now being waved forward. Adel followed closely behind, "Don't look at him." she instructed Clyde as they approached the military style policeman. But out of the corner of his eye, Clyde could see he was about to stop them. Without warning, Adel accelerated and overtook the Toyota, weaving back in front of the larger car. Looking over his shoulder, Clyde could see the man waving his arms frantically. Then they turned the corner and were lost from view. "The secret police are in charge of the traffic control." Adel advised him as they slowed again. "They are Islamic fundamentalists and any woman not wearing a Yashmac is taken into Hasbolla Square for questioning and re-education.

Adel slowed and pulled up at the hotel car park. "I'll collect you here at 6:30pm tonight." Holding the door of the fiat open, Clyde bent and studied her for a few moments, not saying anything. "Cahlede is the seventh son of a seventh son and has the gift of deep insight into things not seen by others." she laughed. "However, I too am aware of your inner thoughts. Beware Infidel; there will be more surprises for you within the ancient world of the Arabian Knights. See you at 6:30pm."

Clyde was at a loose end; he had 4 hours to kill before Adel was to collect him. He wandered around the local shops near the hotel trying desperately to interest himself in the happenings; the clamour and bustle of Arab traders, each trying to sell over the top of each other, or sitting drinking dark, strong coffee from small brass thimble shaped cups. It was pointless, his mind constantly wandered back to Adel. How could she know what he felt? Was Cahlede really able to see into his soul? His practical common sense told him no. But then, did she know, could he see?

Now he entered a dark shop full of woven baskets, carved arte-facts, carpets and rugs. Amongst it all, hanging on a wooden rail, he found a huge recurve hunting bow. It had a polished hand grip bound with copper, each leg of the amazingly thick bow laminated with native iron. The string, once of goat sinews, had been replaced with a synthetic woven silk string. A leather quiver hung with the bow along with 9, 1 metre long, arrows. He picked out one of the arrows eyeing it carefully, it was beautiful. An ivory piece made from camels teeth held the goose feather at the nock end. At the other end, a handmade steel blade with hoed edges, dull from the temper, again fixed to an ivory transition piece. Not a fraction did the shaft bend or twist; straight as a die from flight to blade. "A bargain." said the dealer over Clyde's shoulder. "This bow is a competition bow from the mountain kingdom of Biralwar, beyond the great desert kingdoms of the royal families. It was used at the last competition to take place before the mountain cat was exterminated. The story goes that the winner died, having put an arrow through the big cat's chest, passing through the length of his body and out at his rear the cat's leap took him onto the man, both died together.

Clyde picked up the bow; its balance was perfect. Slowly he pulled back the string between his fingers, back, back until his lips touched the string. A sighting peg of ivory had been fixed to the bow just above the copper hand grip – he could see the cat leap – the draw weight was a heavy 120lbs or more; he could feel the vibrancy within the bow. He relaxed the string gently; the bow regained its nesting shape, "How much?"

"A very rare piece this one, Effendi, unique indeed. Not another one in the whole of Tripoli!" Clyde looked at the dark black Arab who laughed. "Can you even use it, Effendi?" the man asked.

Clyde looked around the shop. At the rear was a long passage leading to a wooden plank door on which hung a small round wreath or dark green leaves. He took an arrow from the quiver, which he turned in his fingers, then placed the nock into the string with the cock feather away from his hand. He guessed the passage to be about 25 yards long – the cat would be 50 or more yards away – slowly he drew back the string once more, this time the bow was loaded. He gently touched the string to his lips; he could feel his heart beat through the string. The ivory sighting peg he placed 6" below the disc, the string slipped easily through his two fingers. In a blur, the shaft sped down the passage and struck the small rosette at the bottom. The cat must have been sighted in at 40 yards he decided. The Arab sucked his teeth noisily as they walked to the door, the steel head had gone completely through the half inch plank and stuck out of the other side about 6 inches. Clyde took hold of the shaft, not exactly sure how he was going to remove it without damage to either the door or the arrow.

"No Effendi, leave the arrow where it is." said the Arab. "And take the bow and remaining arrows with my blessing. I doubt that even the winner could have used this weapon with more accuracy." The Arab rummaged about at the rear of the shop before holding up a leather case, just over a meter long, made of tanned hide and stitched in sinew. "This case came with the bow," he said, "but it is too small to take the bow." Clyde smiled and bent the huge bow to release the string from the wide flattened curve at the end of the arm. Taking hold of the grip and the top arm, he turned it – with a jerk it started to unscrew. Now in two pieces, the bow slid into a compartment within the case, the remaining 8 arrows slid into another side along with the quiver. Clyde closed the lid and tied it down wit the leather thong. At one side was a handle made from laminated ivory and copper, the copper bright green from verdigri. He picked up the case by the handle, it looked completely innocuous, a simple leather case to the unsuspecting eye. He took a 100 rial note from his wallet and handed it to the Arab. The Arab placed both his hand against Clyde's extended one and pushed it back towards him. "The bow is meant for you Effendi – take it. It is a privilege to have seen it used with such skill."

CHAPTER 44

CLYDE SHOWERED AND SHAVED, AGAIN putting on a pair of grey casual trousers and blue shirt. At 6:00pm he went down to the foyer of the hotel. Earlier he had noticed a sign to the health studio and after enquiring at the reception found that it included a gym. "Would you like an instructor?" asked the receptionist.

"No, thank you" replied Clyde, "Can you tell me the hours for the gym?"

"24 hours a day." came the reply.

With that, Clyde wandered into the bar and ordered a beer. Standing at the bar, he tried to analyse his feelings – he had to focus on what he had come to Libya for. As well as his search for Vanessa's killer, he had to find out as much as possible about operation Burning Torch to make sure it was shutdown. He was convinced that McCracken had indeed killed Vanessa and was determined to avenge her. Adel was another distraction, again interrupting his thoughts; she had completely taken him by surprise. He saw her enter the bar from a mirror off to one side of him. She was wearing a one piece reddish brown cat suit and her long hair was tied up in a red handkerchief. As she approached silently, he turned to greet her.

"Hi," she stopped and smiled, "ready to go?"

He drained his glass, "Lead the way." he said.

The house of Ali Akram Jalude's was in the same street as Hassan Gahamahl. The three of them sat on the front bench seat of the green and yellow Ford Transit van which was blazoned down each side with green letters 'Imperial Washing Machine Parts'. Assam drove Adel in the middle and Clyde at the outside. As they drove slowly down the tree lined avenue Assam nodded towards a high white wall, in the centre were large wooden doors 8' high, several strands of razor tape topped the white painted wall. "That's Gahamahl's house." he said. 250 yards further in was a large low Moorish style house set on 5 acres. Palm trees and shrubs concealed the ground between the house and the road, the grass was long and unkept. Originally the house had been unfenced and the lawns ran gently down to the road. Now rolls of razor tape (barbed wire with razor sharp cutting edges along its length) developed in South Africa fenced off the house from the road.

"What does that say?" asked Clyde as they passed a sign covered in Arabic writing.

"Keep out. This is the house of an enemy of the people who was executed for crimes against the state."

"Where do you live now?" enquired Clyde.

"In the old quarter near the Azzawiyah, the old walled city of Biblical times, come we have people to meet." Assam sped up their passage.

The van sped through into the old quarter, the narrow streets were choked with people, oxen, donkey's and dogs. Progress got slower and slower. "Even the secret police have difficulty getting in here." said Adel.

"Not from what I have seen." replied Clyde. His comment went unchallenged.

The van pulled onto a piece of ground where a building had recently been demolished, the debris roughly spread to form a hard standing area. "OK." said Assam, "We are here." Clyde got out and turned to help Adel. She took his hand and stepped out, he held the hand just a faction longer than was necessary, she squeezed it gently and he let it go. Across the narrow street were a row of stone cottages, Assam knocked on the plank door of one of them with a grill placed at eye level. A door slid across and someone looked out. Immediately, bolts were undone and the door opened allowing them inside. Clyde had to duck his head to pass through the door but was amazed at the size of the room that he entered. It was enormous, several cottages must have been knocked down into one, and the stone floor had been polished and shone dully. Goat skin rugs and Persian carpets lay everywhere. Beautiful polished olivewood stools and small tables where scattered throughout. The walls were hung with silk embroidered wall hangings all the way to the rafters giving the impression of a spacious tent. At one end of the long room a group of men sat around a table, Clyde recognised one of them as Cahlede, who rose and came to greet them.

"Hello again," Cahlede said as he shook Clyde's hand. "I hear you have acquired a competition bow."

Clyde stared at him bemused, "Your information is good."

Touching his forehead, Cahlede didn't speak for a few seconds before he burst in laughter. "I am the finest bowman in Libya. Mahood, the dealer who gave you the bow, has shown your arrow to a great many people. Many of these have told me the story. Did you bring the bow with you?"

"No." replied Clyde.

"Such a pity." said Cahlede. "A great pity indeed, we must shoot together, you and me before you return."

"What of the other, Infidel?" asked Assam. One of the other men rose from the floor, "This is Achmed." said Assam, and he shook Clyde's hand vigorously. "He was taken to the Peoples Conference Centre and was there for two hours."

"Who did he meet there?" enquired Clyde.

Assam took hold of his arm, "Please sit." he said as he squatted on the floor cross legged. He indicated a small stool; Clyde pulled it to him and sat down.

"It would appear that several leading figures are here to meet with this man, Edward Chetzway of the African National Congress, George Moffola of Mozambique's Central Committee, Rodriguez Georges of Portugal's Revolutionary Peoples Army, Quan Quay Lok of the Japanese Red Army, Abdulla Hadram of he Islamic Peoples Revolutionary Committee and there are also three others we are yet to identify. The meeting was chaired by no other than our old friend Hararum Samoor, the Chief of Kaddafi's Ministry of Overseas Covert Operations, Foreign Office in other words."

"It would appear that another meeting is scheduled for Monday at Hassan's house." added Assam.

"Monday next?" said Clyde.

"Yes," said Assam, "4 days away."

"All these men have condemned themselves by their actions. All are dedicated to ruthless terrorism to reinforce their beliefs and enforce their will on innocent, and often helpless, people. I for one feel that the world would be a distinctly better place without them. By their actions, they have forfeited the right to remain in society."

Clyde took in all that Assam had said in silence. "We believe that his collection of the world's worst terrorist leaders, some already in power, is planning a central fund to finance further bloodshed and misery. The man I have been following is known to have killed 20 people personally, maybe more, one of which was my sister. I am in agreement with Assam. Have any plans been made to carry out what has been decided?"

"The only way to be sure, would be a bomb in the room in which they meet." said Cahlede. "But this is only 4 days away making it a nearly impossible task. Firstly, we cannot be sure which room it will be held....."

"In a house there cannot be many rooms which would be suitable surely?" interjected Clyde. "I will go to the house and see for myself."

CHAPTER 45

AHLEDE CLIMBED INTO THE CAR with Clyde and Assam drove them to Lakrah Avenue, parking under a tamarind tree at the top of the street. "Do you want me to accompany you?" Cahlede asked Clyde.

Clyde considered this for a moment before replying "No, best I go alone."

Assam took out a small laser pointer from the dash box and handed it to Clyde. "Flash 2 times when you are ready to be picked up, good luck Infidel." Clyde left the car wearing a long dirty over garment with a hood covering his face.

Clyde swiftly walked to the house of Jalood next to the Gahamahl house and squeezed through the front barrier; the grounds were still and quiet. He went behind the shrubbery flanking the house; he could see the electronic wires feeding the closed circuit TV cameras mounted on the wall where its razor tape rolls ended. Reaching the end of the side wall, he peered along the rear boundary; to his amazement the rear boundary was unprotected. High powerful flood lights were mounted on poles lining the boundary of the rear; each with its own motion detector. Obviously they felt that any intruder entering this way could be adequately dealt with under the bright illumination.

Studying his surrounding, Clyde could see that bushes had grown along the concrete wall at the rear boundary since the lights had been installed leaving him access to the house without setting off the motion detectors. He decided, with care, he could use the protection of the wall and bushes to make his way to the house being mindful of the light poles and their detectors.

Now was the test, was the house wired? He examined the windows, as he suspected, the security was on the outside perimeter only, the windows were not wired. Taking a thin blade from his belt pouch, he inserted it into the crack at the opening edge – click, the latch released. Slowly he opened the window. Throwing a leg over the sill, he stepped into the room. Taking a pocket torch from his belt pouch, he looked around the room, which was obviously an office. Just then, a noise came from the desk in the corner of the room. The fax machine had sprung to life. Clyde's conditioned body started, and his adrenalin level rose. Quickly he went to the door and turned the knob – locked – Damn.

The door lock was an old fashioned plate lock and Clyde could see the key was still in the door. He took a piece of paper from the desk, slid it under the door and pushed the key out the other side with a steel pin from his belt pouch. He heard the key hit the wooden floor and carefully pulled the paper back under the door. The key was not on it – Shit. He took the bunch of key picks from the belt pouch and 15 seconds later the door was open.

Cautiously Clyde entered the room which opened into a black and white chequered entrance hall, a large polished staircase curved round and lead up to a gallery. There were 4 doors leading off the hall. At the far side, a passage ran away to the rear of the house. He could hear voices coming from what he imagined to be the servants quarters, and the click of counters on a wooden board. To his right were large double doors with brass handles. He crossed the floor and turned the handles silently, the doors opening into a large room lined with books. The centre of the room was filled with a large high table surrounded by 20 chairs, this had to be it. Clyde took another look into the empty hall and closed the door behind him.

After scanning the room, Clyde crawled underneath the table, taking the package from his jacket he spread the contents on the polished floor – half a kilogram of Semtex, which looked like plasticine, and a small detonator which Assam had supplied. The detonator was no larger than a pen top, along the side was a small screen. As he turned the end, the numbers on the screen glowed eerily to life. Quickly he set the timer to 14:00-90.2.23 – done. It was set for 2:00pm tomorrow, he pushed the end and the flashing stopped – armed. Placing the small tube on the Semtex, Clyde carefully moulded it in his hand to a rough sausage shape.

Holding his torch in his mouth, Clyde directed his attention to the under side of the table. The ancient craftsman, who had hand crafted this oak table, had glued a fillet to join the two side skirts of the priceless piece. Gently he pressed the grey sausage behind and squeezed it into the corner, making sure it was firm. He surveyed his work and was satisfied it wouldn't be seen by a casual glance. Tomorrow, no today, at 2:00pm on this 23rd February, the charge in the slim tube would transfer its energy to the Semtex and Vanessa would finally be avenged. Several other men would also meet their maker, saving the world from countless misery. Clyde felt good. His watched showed this had taken him 25 minutes.

The first part of his task complete, Clyde now took a deep breath as he headed to the door. Placing his ear against its surface he could hear voices and footsteps on the tiled floor outside. Desperately he flashed the torch across the room, searching for a place to hide. He heard the door to the next room, where he had first entered, open and the voices continued. The damned fax machine he thought. Moving to the windows on the far side of the room, he looked out onto the terrace. There stood two guards, at the far end, with a dog, a Rottweiler. Then he saw another window and realised it was covered with wooden panelling – it was obviously the other window he had seen when he entered. Carefully he opened the shutter; it was indeed the window he had seen at the end of the house. Very cautiously, he opened it and stepped out.

Now he must close the window, to be sure that his operation was not even slightly suspected. Sweat broke out on his forehead. Up to now he had been very lucky, he must not rush. He paused and sucked in the heavily scented night air, clearing his brain. Gently he pulled the wooden shutters together, placing the brass latch in the mortise – click, they closed. Pushing up the latch until it just balanced, he closed the window, just before it shut completely, he bumped it firmly felling the latch and the window was closed. Staying low, he crept past the window to the end of the house and glanced up across the terrace, the guards had gone. Quickly he crossed the grass and ducked behind the terrace looking back across the lawn. All was quiet. It was now 45 minutes since he had left the car.

Retracing his entry he was soon back on the road outside the Jalood house. Taking out the laser, he flashed it twice to indicate he was back. Having seen the green speck flash twice, Assam slowly drove up, without actually stopping, opened the door and Clyde jumped in. "Go." he said to Assam with a grin.

CHAPTER 46

THE TEAK PANELLED DOOR OPENED and an Arab servant walked quickly through and headed straight the head of the table speaking briefly with Hassan before leaving. Hassan said to Sean, "You are wanted on the phone, please take it in the library." Sean left the room. He was seated at the green leather topped desk speaking to a flat in Northern Ireland when the Semtex blew. He felt a violent shake as the door blew open, followed by a blast of dust filled air. Knowing instantly what had happened, he instinctively dropped to the floor and crossed himself. For what seemed an eternity, there was silence, in reality it was no more that 2 or 3 seconds.

Sean stood and walked to the door. Across the tiled hall, where the panelled wall used to be, was now a tangled heap of wood, brick and rubble, dust hung in the air, the whole of that side of the house was in ruins. The force of the blast had gone upwards into the first floor and out through the sliding doors. Above, the force had blown out the bedrooms and travelled through these rooms, taking out the roof. Sean could see blue sky beyond the smashed timber framing.

He had been involved in many such explosions but this was the first one in which he had no prior knowledge. As the devastation and damage came home to him, he felt elation. He could smell the acid smell of the explosives but he took comfort in the knowledge that his extraordinary luck had saved him again.

A black and bloodied raggedy arm draped over a sheet of polished panel. He studied it; two fingers were missing and the grey dirt settled on it masking the blood. A white robed servant came from the rear of the house into the hall and stood in shocked amazement at what he saw in front of him. For a few minutes they stood, staring at the massive destruction; the massive amounts of debris and the grey white dust settling. Sean turned to the man, "Where are the car keys?" The man looked puzzled and shrugged. "The motor car." he said slowly going through the movements of starting a car and driving the steering wheel. Understanding now, the servant gestured Sean to follow him and went to the rear of the house. Out the back was a brick paved courtyard with several expensive cars parked there. The servant led him to a dark blue Mercedes and opened the door. Sean could see that the keys were in the ignition.

Jumping into the driver's seat, Sean turned the key and the 5 litre engine caught. He put the gear lever into drive and sped off down the drive, leaving the servant standing there. He slowed to a stop at the large steel gates but the little building that housed the guards was empty. They must have run up to the house on hearing the explosion. He went inside to the control panel to let himself out, but all the controls were written in Arabic.

There was a mass of flick switches on the panel and Sean flicked each of them in turn until the third one opened the gates. Still running on his amazing in-built survival instincts, he drove through the gate and stopped on the other side, returning to the gatehouse. Locating the switch to close the gates, he ran out and jumped into the car, the gates clicked smoothly closed behind him.

A few miles along the road to Tripoli, he passed a yellow transit van with green lettering on the sides, completely unaware of the significance of it and its occupants.

CHAPTER 47

Jack booked a flight with Pegasus Travel; they arranged a hotel in Boston and rental car for his 3 week stay. He arrived at Boston airport on flight PA507. At the Avis desk, he signed the forms and insurance agreement, then a bright young thing in a red and navy uniform with a short skirt dangled a key with a large plastic fob. "Have a nice stay in our beautiful country." she drawled.

A six lane highway took him to the Boulevard where he was booked into the Maple Leaf Motel; Chalet no 47 overlooked the pool. Jack tipped the porter $5 and looked around the room. The chalets were designed to serve as self catering units if required, a full a-la-carte restaurant being available within the complex if you preferred. Each unit was fully equipped with a television, microwave, fridge, cooker etc. Picking up the telephone he dialed 001 and was connected to general enquiries. "Can you tell me where the New Army of God is holding their prayer meetings?" he enquired.

"Hold the line a mo," came the drawl down the line.

Then another voice came on the line, "Plan you day the Godly way! Can I help you?"

Jack repeated the question.

"Hold the line a minute please." and a new recording clicked on.

"The New Army of God will commence enlightenment and promoting the word of the Lord on the 18th day of this month at their temporary assembly hall at Gods little acre in Temple house Park."

The brittle voice continued. "Meetings will commence at 7:30pm every Monday, Wednesday, Friday & Sunday. The very Reverend Master of enlightenment, Algernon Godleman, is available for special consultations between 10:00am and 12noon on the same days. You may call 022-3518 for an appointment." The recording clicked off.

"Get what you wanted honey?" the first voice asked.

"Yes, thank you." replied Jack. "Goodbye."

Jack lay on the bed in deep thought, today was the 17th.

Slowly he drove into Temple house Park, a 2000acre recreation centre for Boston residents. Along the footpath a constant trickle of joggers', skate boarders' and roller skaters' ran, bounced and rolled. A large sign on the path read 'for the New Army of God Assembly Hall' with an arrow pointing the way. The signs were every 100yards or so. At God's little acre (a large playing field size piece of emerald green grass) stood a large marquee about 150yards by 100yards. On the top of a flag pole fluttered a blue and whit flag with a large blue cross on a white background, around the edge were the words 'New Army of God' in blue letters. To one side of the grassed area was a dirt car park sufficient for about 1000 cars. Jack pulled up the green Ford and walked over to the entrance of the huge tent.

At the entrance was a small lobby with high class notice board of oak timber running down both sides. Behind the glass paneling of these boards were photographs. Jack examined them, most were of a large heavy man with black wavy hair; in between the photographs were letters from all over America, Europe and Australia. Jack read a few lines; they all had the same theme, extolling the virtues and praising 'Algernon – God's magnificent messenger', and notes of contributions to the revival fund. He moved his eyes to look into the massive marquee; it was completely full of plastic chairs, row upon row of them. At the far end was a raised dais behind which was another annex similar to the entrance lobby, only much larger. The place was completely empty, not a soul in sight. Jack walked back to his car and drove back to the motel.

CHAPTER 48

Tᴴɪꜱ ᴡᴀꜱ ɴᴏᴛ Jᴀᴄᴋꜱ ꜰɪꜱᴛ visit to America, it was however his first to Boston. Previously he had visited Washington and New York. The first visit had been to a massage parlour in New York which he enjoyed tremendously, 'Eve's'. It was located in a basement under Ralph Tapoles genuine all American style beef steak hamburger bar. On his first visit he had selected a girl called 'Bo Peep' from the 8 or 9 girls available. After his third visit with her he had persuaded Bo Peep, whose real name was Ann Shepherd, to have dinner with him. From that visit to the end of his trip, he had had private massages in his hotel bedroom at very reasonable rates.

Boston was very different to New York. There was no massage parlours listed in the Yellow Pages and none that he could find in the newspapers. Back in his room Jack looked up Ann Shepherd's number in his telephone book, knowing the best time to catch her was before 11:00am. At the third ring a voice answered, "Hi, Ann speaking." They had developed a relationship on Jack's first visit and got even closer on his 2ⁿᵈ; she sounded really pleased to hear from him. The airfare was only $250 for her to fly to Boston and at Jack's request she agreed to come the next day and stay for a few days. Jack waited the next day at the airport; he stood at the barrier watching the people trickling through. She saw Jack before he noticed her and waved and shouted to attract his attention. Ann was not an outstanding looking girl but she had a quality which seemed to Jack irresistible; always alive and bursting with enthusiasm. At no time during the 2 dozen or so times she had been with Jack had she been anything other than excited.

She flung her arms around him oblivious to the other people milling around. "How are you?" she asked breathlessly, "How nice to see you again, how long are you here for, why didn't you come to New York?"

Jack laughed as she carried on without allowing him to answer. When she drew breath he answered with a smile, "I'm good, and I'm here for a seminar being held by a drug company. How are you, you're looking great?"

Ann was 35 years old, divorced without children, but her style made her appear in her early twenties. "Oh, can't complain" she said laughing.

"Business good?" Jack asked with another laugh.

She punched him in the arm, "I can always fit you in, you know that."

He took the small travelling bag and she linked her arm through his as they made their way out of the airport to the car park. From a little distance, they looked like father and daughter. Closer up they looked like lovers, there was no way they looked like hooker and client.

Jack had never told Ann anything about his life in England, she knew he was married and owned a chemist shop but that was the extent of her knowledge. Their relationship did not need long discussions on his background, she was happy to perform her skills for him and share the time to enjoy some of his spending sprees at fancy restaurants. Each time Jack had left before she had felt sad for a while as she genuinely enjoyed his company. Her life was full of shallow relationships with sad, and often, peculiar people. And even if it was pretend, Jack was different from the everyday. He sent her presents on her birthday and at Christmas, and each time he left, at the Chase Manhattan Bank, she had deposited $1500 toward her retirement fund. He decided not to involve Ann in his present situation, Bernard was not going anywhere, and he would enjoy his Bo Peep for a few days.

CHAPTER 49

"Ow long will you be in the hair salon?" he enquired.

"Oh, only two or three hours." she grinned.

"OK, I'm going out for a while; I'll be back at 8:30pm. The table is booked at Sandies for 9:00pm."

As Jack approached Gods Little Acre he could see that the car park was almost full, 5 or 6 attendants with flashlights were directing cars into orderly lines. Jack parked in the space indicated and walked towards the brightly lit marquee. At the entrance long queue, two & three wide, fed into the lobby, it took a few minutes to get up to the dozen or so people who lined the entrance handing out leaflets. Jack took one from a pallid young girl of about 20 who was saying, "Welcome to God's transit lounge, please pass through into the hall and find a seat. Gods messenger starts at 7:30pm sharp."

Jack sat at the end of a row of seats near the back. Up in the roof, 6 high lights illuminated the massive tent. It filled rapidly with all manner of people – old, young, rich, poor, male and female – the whole seating area was now full and people were now standing between the seats and the tent walls. And still they came until the tent was packed from one end to the other. Between Jack's seat and the wall nearest to him, people stood shoulder to shoulder 15 or 20 deep. Suddenly a hush descended, all the lights went out and the stage was illuminated.

Though Jacks purpose for being here was very different from the vast majority of those present, he couldn't help himself feeling in awe of the man who strode onto the stage at the far end of the tent. It was obvious who he was, over the door to the rear annex hung a 15' high poster with his full length portrait on it. From everywhere, a loud fanfare of trumpets sounded. Jack looked up and noticed the large loud speaker boxes fixed to the tops of the long tent poles holding the annex. The man on stage held up his arms and the fanfare ceased, "Welcome to the Lords Transit Lounge." the voice boomed over the loud speakers. "Join me in prayer." He knelt down on the stage, still holding his arms up in the air. The entire congregation, which had stood at his entrance, now sank down to their knees while Jack returned to his seat. "Oh Lord, make this meeting fruitful this evening." his mesmeric voice filled the tent, on and on.

Jack studied the stage. Behind the kneeling Algernon were 4 people; 2 women, an elderly man with white hair and another man who was thin, with short cropped wispy hair who sat on a chair with his head bowed. Jack wondered if this could be the object of his search. With a start, Jack realized the man had stopped praying and had risen, the congregation rose too. "Please be seated." he directed and those that could did.

"Today I have with me living proof of God's infinite mercy and forgiveness. You see before you tonight a miserable sinner who until a few days ago was serving a jail sentence in England. Until he turned to the Lord his worthless life was without purpose or direction, drifting endlessly in and out of sin and degradation. Now Brother Bernard has joined me on this crusade for the Lord. Stand up Brother Bernard," Algernon shouted, "stand up and give testimony to his infinite wisdom and mercy in pardoning you and setting you up in righteousness, sending you forward to proclaim him Lord." Slowly the man stood up, uneasy and furtive. Algernon passed him a microphone.

"I have sinned against the Lord," the man whined in a broad Yorkshire accent, "I have repented and been forgiven."

"Thank you Brother Bernard," Algernon shouted, "Proof indeed of what can be done when you believe, when you truly repent."

Jack had seen enough, he had located what he had travelled to Boston for. Now he had to do two things to satisfy himself of Bernard's guilt then destroy him with as little fuss as possible.

At the end of the service, Algernon put his arm around Bernard and together they walked through the crowds to the entrance, pushing and jostling with the congregation, many patting Bernard on the shoulder and back encouraging him in his new found faith.

CHAPTER 50

ASSAM STARTED THE CAR AND headed towards Tripoli. Clyde was silent, lost in thought. "Collect your things tonight Infidel," he said, "Tomorrow we are going to take you into the desert for a while. My family still own a large estate at the Kufra Oasis, beyond the great Sand Sea. We have sent word to say we are coming and bringing an important guest." Clyde glanced sideways at Assam who smiled. "Adel will be going as well." he said laughingly. Clyde stared out the window, saying nothing.

Assam collected Clyde at 7:30am the next morning in a white four wheel drive truck. On the back were three 3 wheel motor bikes with balloon like tyres. Clyde threw his bag into the back and climbed up beside Cahlede. "Hello again, Infidel." He greeted Clyde with a smile. "Well, I must say, you have made quite a mess of Hassam's splendid residence, have you not?" He opened a newspaper showing Clyde the front page photo picture of the damaged room which had been taken from the hall.

"What does it say about the people killed?" questioned Clyde.

Cahlede read from the paper. "A large explosion last night wrecked a cabinet minister's house and killed a number of important international leaders. It is thought to have been engineered by the American CIA government department. Investigations are underway into this terrible outrage against freedom movements." Cahlede stopped.

"Is that all?" Clyde enquired. "Nothing about who was killed?"

"No, they will not release those details for some time after."

"To more important matters now, did you bring the bow?"

"Yes, it's in the back"

"Good, then you can compete in day three." said Cahlede. Clyde looked puzzled. Turning to Assam, "Have you not told him?"

"No." he replied.

"What is going on?" asked Clyde.

"The competition starts two days after we arrive at Kufra." Cahlede went on.

"What competition, can someone tell me what's going on please?" asked the still puzzled Clyde.

Cahlede explained. "As far back as anyone can remember, the first week in March, every five years, has been reserved for the competition; a trial of strength and stamina for the desert warriors. The event is held over three days with three separate disciplines thus allowing competitors who excel in one or more disciplines to notch up points. The event culminates into the greatest event of all, the bow shoot. This is followed by three days of feasting and enjoyment. I have taken the liberty of nominating you as head of the house of Ali-Akram Jalude as our entry for this year. Each family, from each region, can nominate only one name. This year, you are to be 1 of 56 competitors. It is a real honour Infidel; very rarely does an outsider get the opportunity to compete."

"And what of you?" asked Clyde.

"Yes, I too am competing; I represent the house of Jalah-Ah-Ban-Makish as my father before me and his father before him did."

Clyde sighed and stared straight ahead at the road in front of them for a few minutes before laughing. "And what, besides the bow, are the other disciplines?" he enquired.

"The first is stamina; competing against oneself. Only the men making it through this first event are winners and able to compete in the second event. More that 50% of competitors do not make the end of the first day. The second day is hand to hand; here the men compete against each other without weapons in unarmed combat. The winners of this go on to compete in the final day of bow competition." Cahlede laughed, "Ah Infidel. At the great Kufra, I guarantee an unknown quantity like you will be attracting long odds on first day survival already."

It took them 4 hours to reach Nafoora, the end of the tar road, where they pulled in and parked behind the ramshackle filling station. Clyde was getting out of the vehicle when he was startled by an old Arab who had run over and began shaking his hand vigorously, chattering away in Arabic. Cahlede was beside himself, laughing. After regaining his composure, he spoke with the old Arab. Turning to Clyde, with a more respectful laugh he said, "It would appear Infidel that many people know of your talents. I suspect the story of the arrow you left stuck in Mamood's door has been exaggerated somewhat."

Also excited by the commotion, Assam broke in, "The odds are not now whether or not you will last day one but whether or not you can win! You see, for the past 7 years the competition has been dominated by a man from Fejjan Province. Consecutively he has beaten all other competitors and has justifiably been surrounded by an air of invincibility. In short, people need to see him beaten and you are an unknown quantity, a hope that you could perhaps beat this man of steel."

"Come Infidel, leave your thoughts of the coming trails of fortitude and help us refuel these sturdy 3 legged mechanical camels." They left Nafoora on the bikes, each loaded up and pulling a small cart behind with fuel and food. They covered 150 miles that first day before camping at the side of the desert trail.

Having lit a fire, they now sat around it as the night grew colder. Clyde was glad of his lightweight sleeping bag. "How long to Kufra?" he asked Assam.

"Tomorrow we meet Adel and other people also going to the competition at Savir. There we will change to the real camels and it is two more days ride to Kufra."

Savir is a small settlement at the western side of the Great Sand Sea, The Libyan Desert. A small collection of houses were scattered around a few wells where water is hand pulled in buckets to the surface.

At a large house with a courtyard, they parked the bikes and dismounted. Several camels were tethered in the courtyard, imperviously chewing and staring into space.

Clyde stood and stretched, it felt good. He knew that somewhere in the house was Adel. Already he could feel his stomach churning and pulse quickening. The front door opened and there she was, coming down the steps, slim and elegant in khaki paratrooper pants and a green blouse. The pants were tucked into polished leather boots. She kissed Assam on the cheek before turning to Clyde. As her eyes met his, he could feel the colour rising from his collar. She smiled, "Hi" she said, her eyes danced and sparkled.

Clyde felt awkward. "Hi yourself." he said "You look lovely."

"Thank you 'Oh Great Competitor', with the green eyes and the pale skin, your unknown prowess has shortened the odds dramatically!"

"Adel, you are embarrassing our guest." Assam said sharply. "Be gone you useless prattle and get us men some food."

"Yes Master, at once." she laughed and turned to go into the house. Hesitating, she placed her hand on Clyde's arm and stared into his eyes. Quietly she said, "I have a feeling about you, you have a great power within you and I know you will win, if you want it. The house of Jalude has never come near to winning the competition but being one of the 8 royal families, we can nominate a champion to compete on our behalf without loss of honour. Perhaps this is hard to understand by outsiders, but that is the traditional law. I know you are the one to be this year's winner." She kissed him lightly on the cheek and was gone.

It was 6:30am the next morning and the courtyard was already hot, the sun having cleared the top of the wall. The fragrant scent of Frangipani blossom wafted in the warm breeze and a camel coughed. They had eaten omelettes and oat cakes with honey washed down with strong Turkish coffee, black, sweet and powerful as servants loaded the camels.

"Have you ever ridden a camel before?" asked Assam of Clyde. Clyde shook his head. "It is easy. There is only one rule to remember, you are the boss. The minute you forget that, the camel will please itself. Noble beasts, willing, untiring and comfortable to ride provided you are in charge." Clyde hoisted himself into the soft leather saddle and the large ungainly animal rocked and swayed as it rose to its feet and grunted.

"You control them like a horse with the reigns and stirrups." he continued as he pulled down violently on the reign hand. The camel's head was forced down and right, the large beast wheeled round and he dug his heel into its side; the animal grunted and trundled off through the open gate. Clyde did the same and the camel responded well, following Assam out of the courtyard. Adel, now wearing a long trim robe, caught up with him. They had given Clyde a long Arab Dress to wear, which he found remarkably comfortable, with a large hood. Adel had told him that once they cleared the settlement he would be glad of the hood as the sand gets everywhere.

In the silence of the desert, Clyde found that talking to Adel was easy, and for hours they chattered. She had spent most of her life in Europe at school, first in England, and then France, only returning to Libya 12 months previously. In the short time Clyde had known her he had regarded her as European rather than Arab, and as he talked with her he realised that she too regarded herself as no longer Arab. For the whole of the day's journey, they talked without a pause, almost oblivious to the other 9 or so travelling companions. At night however, they were forced to mix with the others. Clyde felt some reluctance to let her go as she helped the other two women prepare the food.

Cahlede and another two of their party walked across the dusty, baked mud area in the centre of the collection of mud brick houses, to a coverall made of sticks which housed several sheep. After a few minutes of trading, the Arab and a boy took one of the sheep behind the small hut and slaughtered it. Unbelievably, returning about 1 hour later with a bundle of sheepskin. Inside the skin was the whole sheep, butchered and deboned.

Heavily seasoned and cut into thin strips, the meat was cooked slowly in large metal pans over the fire. This was eaten with flat bread, baked crusty on the same pan as the meat. Clyde helped himself to a drink, pouring from a large canteen jug into the small vessels set out on the white table cloth on the ground. The liquid was slightly tart, almost like yoghurt. He looked at Assam with a query in his expression. "Palm wine and goat's milk." he grinned. "Good for stamina."

From across the fire Adel was looking at Clyde the fire dancing in her dark eyes. She got up and walked around to his side and sat down on the rugs. As she sat, he could feel her close to his thigh and a shudder ran through his body. He could smell fresh Jasmine. At first he stared into the flames, unsure how to deal with his emotions, the easy chatter of the day now far away, almost like a dream. Slowly he turned to her, just as she looked up at him, neither spoke for a moment and then, "You know, don't you?" his whispered hoarsely.

"Yes." she nodded slightly. "Yes." she said again, almost inaudibly. "Nothing will ever be the same now. In all my life I have never met a man to make me feel like this." As Clyde stared down into the depths of her dark eyes, the flames danced yellow, red and orange, her lips parted and her white teeth showed. He slowly bent to kiss the lips. She placed a finger on his chin, "Not now," she breathed, "Later."

Slowly the chatter returned to his conscious mind, he was again aware of the others. A camel grunted across the yard. Across the fire Assam's face came into focus and he grinned an open grin, he also knew. Assam liked the Irishman and respected him. In the short time they had known each other; he had quickly assessed his skills and integrity. He acknowledged that his sister was devastatingly attractive but the Irishman was the first he had seen her show any real interest in. In Europe she had never been short of escorts, boyfriends came and went, but nothing serious. Clyde settled back and took in the quiet chatter before calling it a night.

Clyde closed his eyes but he couldn't sleep. In the silence of the night he could hear the desert sounds, tiny rustling - Gecko's in the rooting, the camel's leather heads creaking, the soft plop of ash falling back into the dying fire. Silently, he slipped his legs out of the sleeping bag and rose to a crouch, the rest were all silent, heavy breathing noises of men at rest. Slowly he stood and walked to the doorway, pausing, his eyes now accustomed to the dark interior of the hut, and glanced back to see no-one moved. It was cold on the hard earth floor. Outside, looking up, he could see an incredible star studded sky. The wind swayed the palm trees across the compound, the green fronds clicked and swished slightly in the breeze. He walked directly to the fire and squatted down beside the faint red ashes, unsure what to do next. His thoughts were interrupted, he knew she was coming to him, even though her hut was across the compound behind him, he could hear her soft footsteps on the hard earth floor. He stood and turned to greet her, goose bumps rising on his arms. He took her gently in his arms placing his lips against hers. He lips were moist and slightly parted and she pressed her whole body hard against his chest. Moving slightly from side to side, with her tongue gently running along his lips, she slid her cold hands under his singlet and ran then up across his back to his shoulder blade. Gently she ran her nails across his bare skin causing him to shudder. As she moved gently, forcing her hips against his body, they both felt it rise – hard and urgent. Freeing herself from his arms, she ran to the hut she had come from returning with a coloured rug which she spread beside the dying fire.

"Let me love you," she whispered, "Arab style." Clyde hugged her to him and inhaled the sweet perfume. As her body senses raced, the jasmine on her skin gave off waves of heady perfume, mingling with the smell of her very essence. His desire was all consuming; he was lost to another world. With clumsy fingers he fumbled to pull down his shorts. Gently she placed her hands over his, and took control of his undressing. Then, lifting the loose cotton shift up to her waist, she settled down onto his legs with her own legs left wide open behind him. Teasingly she slid slowly along his legs toward him, wrapping her arms behind his back. Carefully, she pulled herself up until they touched. As Clyde entered her, she shuddered, covering his mouth with her own.

After the initial rush of passion had passed, they sat on the rug holding each other tightly. Clyde held her shoulders, looking deep into her eyes. Tears welled in the dark eyes and trickled slowly down her beautiful cheeks. "What is it?" asked Clyde tenderly.

"Oh my sweet," she breathed, "how can there ever be a future for us – we come from such different worlds?"

Clyde felt his elation and feelings of fulfilment slip away and a great, grey depression settled upon him. He stared over her into the darkness, past the palm trees into the great desert. "I will not let you go." he said turning back to her, "Not now." The moment had passed and they were both feeling depressed. They sat for another hour without speaking, each thinking of the future.

CHAPTER 51

THEY ARRIVED AT KUFRA THE next day about 2:00pm. Clyde had decided that whatever the cost, he would persuade Adel to leave Libya with him. How he would accomplish this he left for later thought. Happy with his decision, his mood had lightened up considerably. Adel too had covered her feminine flippancy and was a fresh and light as spring flowers, as if she had also made a great decision and left the details to the great god of change and tomorrow. As they rode side by side toward the place marking the edge of the Great Sand Sea, he looked across at her and was happy to see her eyes sparkled again. "Last night," he said, "was……."

"Oh Infidel, last night" she took over his conversation as he paused, "was the beginning, not the end. It is just the details that are left to sort out. I have a surprise waiting for you at the house of Ali-Akram Jalude. Can you ride a horse?" she enquired, smiling.

"Yes." replied Clyde. "When I was first in the army, one of my close friend's fathers managed a Polo Club in Scotland owned by the Haudam brothers, the United Arab Emirates horse mad Arab family. Every pass out we got we spent there riding through the mountains in the Cairngorms in Central Scotland. Why do you ask?"

"The first day of the great games is completely horsemanship." she replied.

"Is that the surprise?" he laughed.

"No, for my 21st birthday, my family gave me the finest horse in the Arab world – bred from 2000 years of Arabian horst mythology – an absolute beauty, black as night – she is a filly of true power and style. You are going to ride her in the great games. Her name is Dark Side of the Moon.

The Kufra Oasis marked the end of the Great Sand Sea and the start of the Ancient Mountain Kingdoms located in the Tibetan Mountain foothills which ran into Northern Chad. Here the water from mountains ran to the surface before it vanished forever, trying to assuage the thirst of the Libyan deserts. From the bustle and throng of the old style town, it was obvious that may others, from all over, have journeyed here. "All here for the games." Armed said, as if in answer to an unspoken question. "This is the highlight of the year." Striped tents, with tasselled initials depicting different tribes, spread out from the palm fringed river. The smell of wood smoke (an unusual smell in Arabia) mingled with the camel and cooking odours. They passed through the main street slowly, the camel patiently plodding forward in their ungainly rock and roll style, which Clyde had grown used to over the journey from Savir.

The town was a mixture of old and new houses. Mainly sunburnt mud brick houses with remarkable clay tiled roofs. As they passed through the main town, the houses spaced further apart and Clyde could see about half a mile ahead. Towards the mountains he could see a number of posts, with flags and pennants fluttering in the hot wind. "The great arena!" Assam said watching Clyde's gaze.

The mountains ran almost to the edge of the town and rose majestically far into the hot brown distance. Great bare rock pinnacles rose out of the green tree clad lower foothills. Again, as if reading his thoughts, Assam spoke as they stopped the camels. "They finally end far away in the forests of Central Chad, a vast wilderness of primitive backward blacks. Our ancestors used to raid beyond these mountains and bring back blacks for slaves, long lines of them chained together and sold to the Egyptians. They were used to build the vast pyramids of the Pharaoh long before America was colonised."

Across the shimmering peaks and down over the trees, a great black eagle soared using the hot air, it glided effortlessly along the tree line. Without warning, as if someone flicked a switch, it dropped a wing and floundered – twisting and turning. Two small dark brown birds with long forked tails and sharp pointed wings had punched upwards from the green canopy to harass and annoy the eagle. 'Whee whee' the strange whistling shriek of the two birds floated down to where they stood. "Lanners" said Assam, "They nest on the rock ledges just above the tree line. Obviously they have young and they will not tolerate the eagles near their nesting site. Come, we have trained Lanners in the mews, I'll show you close up how fierce the little falcons are."

Clyde was reluctant to move, he stared at the eagle. The great bird rose, almost vertically, with the two little falcons close on his tail. Higher and higher he soared, coming closer over where they stood. Clyde could clearly see the eagle's yellow beak now, long and thick with its top mandible hooked over, a great heavy weapon, and the two small lanners sleek and fast; he was fascinated with the drama. 'Aee Aee' the great black bird rolled at the top of his climb and allowed the two smaller birds, unable to check, to go past as he did so. His great feathered legs shot out with his yellow toes spread, the hooked tips clearly visible. Now upside down, one swoop of his wings and the claws punched the air just inches behind one of the lanners. The two broke off the attack and streaked down to the tree line. The eagle righted himself and floated majestically away down along the line of the river.

CHAPTER 52

"WELCOME TO THE HOUSE OF Ali-Akram Jalude." said Assam as he slid off his camel with a flourish.

"I thought Arabs roamed about the desert in tents." said Clyde keeping a straight face. "The house looks new, how long has this been your family seat?"

Assam looked crestfallen. No longer able to contain himself, Clyde burst into laughter at Assam troubled face.

While Clyde recovered himself, Assam went on to explain. "In the old days each of the 8 royal families had a vast tract of land to look after, but every year at this time they all gathered here for the games. Where this house now stands was my family's traditional site to make camp." They dismounted and tethered the camels and headed towards a door in the courtyard.

The front of the house faced the river, green lawn, somewhat incongruous, ran down to the river. A large paved area at the rear of the house was covered by striped awnings done to resemble the traditional tent. Rugs, cushions and small padded stools were dotted around huge fronded palms in earthen pots standing between the gaily coloured, sweeping awnings and the lawns. The rear of the house was a complete sliding glass wall, each 2m section sliding behind the next, to open up the house to the outside area, or close it off to allow the air conditioning to cool down the inside of the house.

"Come and meet the rest of my family." Clyde followed Assam into the house. The inside was as opulent as the outside.

"This is my mother, Lamier." Assam stood to one side of a woman and Clyde could instantly see where Adel got her poise and beauty. A lady of great elegance and presence, she extended her hand and Clyde took it in his. It was firm and dry. "I am pleased to meet you." she said. Clyde was surprised at the quality of her voice, beautiful, educated and allured tones. She smiled, "I am, or was, very English." she said, "County set from Surrey."

"I'm sorry." apologised Clyde. "I didn't expect you to be........" he hesitated.

"So English." she finished for him laughingly. "30 years ago I married Mamood and took on the role of an Arab wife. I have loved every minute from that day until the day he died. Since he was killed I have taken his mantle and with my two eldest boys, Hamaadri and Ramdah, we run the family firm. While these two" she indicated Adel and Assam "attempt to undermine the regime that executed their father, with a little help from the firm." She clapped her hands and a servant appeared through a door, bowing slightly. "Show our guest to his room. I'm sure you would like to shower and change." she said to Clyde. "Please join us in the garden when you are ready."

Clyde followed the silent Arab servant down the passage to his room, it was huge. A great bed took up the whole of one wall - hanging drapes turned it into a feature, skins and rugs covered the cool floor. A large fan spun lazily from the ceiling. The bathroom lead off a small annex, completely tiled in marble, the wash hand basin and shower were black, the toilet was also the same black china, the opulence was breathtaking.

The family had gathered in the garden. "I hear he has many admiral qualities." Lamier said to Assam. He smiled and looked at his sister who blushed violently. Lamier noticed this but said nothing.

"He indeed has qualities that are difficult to explain." Assam said to his mother. "He has a kind of reliability not easy to define."

"What are his chances at the games?" she asked.

Assam shrugged, "He has acquired a kind of aura since he got this competition bow in Tripoli. I have not seen him in action but we both have a feeling about him." he said including Adel who agreed. "He's going to ride Dark Side of the Moon." she added.

"Since your uncle died, the firm has lost face in the competition. It is time to put things right, we need to gain face again with the other 7 families."

Assam stood as Clyde came across the tiled floor. Clyde's skin had darkened from the sun on their journey, apart from his green eyes, he could have passed for an Arab. "Are you fully refreshed Infidel?"

"Fully charged." replied Clyde.

"Then come join us, I will show you the true sport of kings."

The birds sat on timber posts with leather padding around the top. There were 8 in total. Two lanner falcons, a peregrine, two eastern banded kites, a crested eagle and a great black eagle. Each bird had its own caged flight area, except the paired birds which were together. Assam opened the door stepped into the cage with the peregrine, the birds fierce yellow eyes turned to watch his approach 'Kee' the bird opened its beak and shrieked at him. He placed a gloved hand beside its feet and it stepped on. He walked to Clyde with the grey striped predator on his gloved fist. The bird had turned its head and its yellow eye stared at Clyde unblinking. "Isn't she beautiful?" sighed Assam. "Omar, meet Clyde. You are two of kind; efficient, ruthless killers." The bird picked up each of its feet in turn, the little bells tinkled as she moved. "Tomorrow we will fly her against the sand grouse."

Later that night as Clyde lay on the bed the words echoed in his head. 'A ruthless efficient killer, Is that what he was? Was that how people who knew him thought of him? Adel, is that how she saw him? No, she couldn't could she? And Assam is that how he truly saw him – like Cahlede?'

It was time to take stock of himself. He had thought of nothing but revenge since Vanessa's murder. Now that he had avenged her by killing 'The Wolf' he still felt no satisfaction – nothing. It seemed as though he had been empty, without purpose, until he had met Adel. Now he wanted to change, no longer satisfied with the skills of violence he wanted the normal things in life. Like a house and children, a future. Was that too much to hope for? He feared it would not be that simple to leave the past behind.

CHAPTER 53

CLYDE HAD RISEN EARLY THE next day and gone for a run along the river. He had travelled about 3 kilometres before returning on the tracks he had already made. Sweat soaked the light green singlet front and back, the sweat from his face and neck running rivulets onto his shoulders, he felt good. As he was approaching the courtyard he could see several servants were preparing horses.

"Morning Clyde." said Assam. "I hope you can ride?"

"I would look pretty useless on the first day of the games if I could not, wouldn't I?" he said with a wry grin.

"Yes, that would be a great disappointment to quite a number of people." Assam replied. "Come, I will introduce you to the one you shall be riding the day after tomorrow." In the second stall of the large stable block was a horse like no other Clyde had seen before. It was as if it had been charged with electricity – Jet black from its nose to its tail – the long plumes of its tail swished. Tethered to the wall with a simple halter, it turned to them nostrils flaring sleek and shiny. "This." he said, "is Dark Side of the Moon." The horse was a beauty indeed. As Clyde stared in awe, he wondered what the cost of such a magnificent animal could be. The beast pranced round on it black legs, its hoofs clattering on the concrete.

Adele came through the stable doors and stood beside Clyde smiling up at him, "What do you think?" she asked.

Clyde had difficulty with his words. "It's a horse in a class of its own, a class beyond anything I've seen, what a looker!" The horse snorted.

"Come and meet her." She opened the stall and Clyde followed her in, the beauty clattered around and whinnied. Adel took hold of the halter and stroked its head, "Hey girl." she said softly. The horse snorted again and nuzzled her. "This man is going to ride you to win; it will be your greatest challenge."

Clyde stroked the smooth muscled rump and ran his hand along her back to the neck. She turned to look at him and Adel stepped back for Clyde to take the halter. He took the horses head in his hands and gently breathed into its nostrils; the horse shook its head up and down. Clyde repeated this move then patted the horse's neck. She replied by nuzzling him.

Adel gave a delighted little laugh, "Oh, I have a good feeling about you, one surprise after another."

"If you agree, I will take her this morning."

"Good idea." Assam interjected.

They fetched a simple Arab saddle onto her back and handed Clyde the reigns. He mounted carefully, feeling each other out, he could feel the great power and vibrancy of the horse. "She's a beauty, absolutely tops." He allowed her to pick her way delicately across the courtyard while leaning over and stroking her powerful neck. In a low voice he slowly talked to the horse. They were strange words, nobody could understand what was said to her but the animal seemed to understand.

"What language was that?" asked Assam.

"Gaelic!" Clyde replied. "It was an old Gaelic phrase on encouragement."

"She only understands Arabic." Assam exclaimed.

"Well, now she understands Gaelic as well." retorted Clyde. "Watch carefully." He again spoke in the strange tongue at the same time gently digging his heels into her. The horse took off like greased lightening and in an instance was 50 metres away, like a black streak. Pulling her up Clyde waited for Assam to catch up.

"Very impressive," he said when he came abreast, "very impressive indeed." On his gloved fist sat Omar with a hood covering her head, the little bells tinkled each time she moved. "Ahmed, pass me the browning." he said to one of the servants. Ahmed passed a Browning 20 bore shot gun to Assam. "Can you use a shot gun as well as all the other weapons you are so proficient in." he asked Clyde. Clyde smiled and he handed him the gun. Clyde put the shotgun to his shoulder and open eyed, stared down the length of it to the little steel blob at the tip of the barrels. He could see all the rib. "The gun will shoot high, a must for rising birds. You will have to be careful though Clyde, the horse has not been shot over before.

They rode slowly along the riverbank; the bush was dense near the bank, gradually thinning out into dry grass. Two pointer dogs worked the dense grasses close to the brush a short distance ahead of the horses. Suddenly the dog nearest the river stiffened, its left front paw raised as if it had frozen in mid stride, its tail stood out stiffly behind. Intently the dog stared into the ground directly in front of him. "Look at the dog Clyde." Assam said softly. "Get ready." Clyde sat relaxed on the horse with the browning at the ready. "Push it out Ramee." he said to the dog who responded by dropping its nose to the ground and taking a step forward. Two brown birds exploded from the grass and rocketed upward. They had risen about 6m and were about 2m apart rising and disappearing rapidly. Clyde followed the left hand birds' imaginary path with the browning, up past the bird and pulled the trigger. Without any hesitation he crossed to the right hand bird, into its path, he pulled the trigger again. At the two reports the birds collapsed into the grass. "Good shooting Clyde." exclaimed Assam.

The black horse had skittered slightly at the earlier shots but Clyde had easily calmed her down. The dog was pointing again. "More birds Clyde?" asked Assam.

"No thanks." replied Clyde. "That's enough with the gun, come on and show me what Omar can do."

Assam slipped off the horse, removed the hawk's hood and slipped the leather thong tying the bells. Omar knew what was ahead and became alert, his yellow eyes flashed. "Push it out Yheel." he said to the second dog and it walked slowly forward. This time it was a sandy coloured bird that burst out of the grass and flew strongly upwards into the blue sky. Assam turned his wrist and threw the falcon into the air. The bird's wings cleaved the air as she strained to make height, up and up she went. Then she saw the fleeing bird, a sand grouse, and rapidly she overhauled it, climbing and climbing. Suddenly she streaked down, her long legs reached out with the hooked talons extended. They could hear the hit 80 yards away. Predator and prey fell together. Racing to the bird, Assam bent and placed the hood over the hawk's head. He took her by the legs and gently stroked the smoke grey back. Taking a small piece of meat from the bag at his waist, he offered it to the bird, almost as a consolation for taking its prize. It had been a good outing.

They were rode slowly back toward the house along the riverbank. Clyde was silent as he was deep in thought about Adel. Could they put it together, how much would they each have to change to make it work? He let the thoughts hang for a while in his head. "Let's see how fast this horse is." he said to Assam.

"Oh, she is good Infidel." Assam replied with a grin.

Clyde dug in his heels and willed the black, vibrant horse forward. Like a tightly coiled spring, the beast took off. It was exhilarating, he could feel the great muscles beneath the shining coat writhing and contracting. He turned the head with the reigns and with his knees towards the riverbank. The horse understood the command and trusted him down the stony band almost to the waters edge, a flat hard baked ledge along the waterline. They sped along this natural path. Ahead a tree branch, as thick as a man's leg, stretched out across the path and over the water. As they hurtled towards it, the horse sensed the branch was too low. "Go, go my beauty" Clyde urged in Gaelic. He lay across and down to the side, leaving only his leg across the horses back. The horse lowered its head and Clyde felt the branch lightly scrub his leg as the galloped beneath the tree.

Assam, who was well behind, saw all that had happened. "Very impressive." he thought to himself. "A well matched pair indeed."

CHAPTER 54

THE HEAD WAITER USHERED THEM politely to a secluded table beside the waterfall and lit the everlasting candle in the red glass bowl, "Enjoy your meal." he said and left. The wine waiter appeared and enquired what they would like; Jack ordered a Gin and Tonic for himself and a Whiskey sour for Ann. The waiter spent a long time looking down Ann's low cut dress before leaving to get the drinks. On his return Jack requested a bottle of Moet "Room 64," he instructed placing his key on the table.

"Yes sir." the man said as he noted the room number on his order pad and stole another look down Ann's cleavage before leaving.

"Perhaps I could fit him in between the main course and dessert, do you think?" she said to Jack with a giggle.

The meal was excellent and they took their time over coffee. Jack motioned the wine waiter over. "Have another bottle of Moet sent to chalet number 64." he said.

"Right away sir." he said with a smirk.

As they walked leisurely past the pool on their way back to the chalet, Ann said "It's twice the price after midnight you know?" Jack looked at his watch; it was 11:55pm. "We'd better hurry then." he said as he broke into a run.

She caught him up and grabbed his arm laughing "OK, OK" she said, "Standard rates for special friends."

The Moet was on the coffee table in an ice bucket with two champagne flutes beside it when they arrived. "Before or after?" said Jack indicating the bottle.

She considered him, then the bottle, "During." she said with a laugh.

They stood looking at each other in the light from the bedside table, which the waiter had switched on when he delivered the Moet. Slowly she took the shoulder straps off, one at a time. The dress slid to the floor and she steeped out of the red circle at her feet and kicked off the red high heeled shoes. She was not wearing a bra and her breasts, though large and heavy, were standing straight out in front, only drooping slightly due to their size; the pink nipples were puckered and stood out. Her tongue peeped out between her lips and moistened them slightly. She walked over to Jack and kissed him slowly on the lips, her tongue probing his mouth. She tasted coffee and mint, her breath was warm and musky.

One by one she unbuttoned his shirt buttons, pulling it out of his trousers as she went. Lifting his shirt at the sides, she took it off and left it hanging on his wrists. She pushed her breasts against his chest and moved slowly from side to side, pushing her hips against him, feeling his trousers bulge as his weapon rose, her hands grasped his hair at the back and forced his face into hers as she sucked at this mouth.

Jack ran his hands down her back and across her hips to his trousers, he undid his belt and they fell to the floor. Her movements became quicker and quicker as she ground her hips against him. He hooked his fingers into his underpants, and standing on one leg pulled them down one leg first and then the other, leaving them around his ankle. Taking hold of her own panties, she pulled them down, bending over as she did. Jack placed his hand on her bottom and slid his hand down her cheeks. She turned toward him, still bent and took his weapon in her mouth. Slowly and wetly she pulled away from him and straightened, leveling her face with his. "That was just a sample," she grinned, "what would my master like next?" With an exaggerated hip sway, she went to the bed and lay upon the over quilt with one leg on top of the other at right angles to her thighs. Jack could see enough to produce goose pimples on his arms and legs. She smiled and held out her arms, "Come on kind sir," she said, "it's long gone midnight, now everything else is a bonus."

The next three days were filled with sex as the pair indulged themselves, eating, making love and drinking, Jack forgetting his reason for being here, Ann forgetting her trade. But as with all things good, the time passed too quickly. They both felt a great loss as Jack said goodbye to Ann.

"Keep in touch." she said as she touched his cheek.

"I will and thank you for your company." Jack placed an envelope in her open shoulder bag. She looked at it and then at Jack, a tear welled in the corner of her eye and ran down her cheek.

"Jack," she said with a catch in her voice, "you don't have to do it this time."

"I know, I know." said Jack. "But I want to, anyway its double time after midnight."

Jack lay on his bed and thought long and hard. He was one of those lucky people who, although he took no exercise to speak of, remained fit and healthy; his body gave the impression of great athletic prowess. Narrow hips and behind made his shoulders look broader than they were. At 38, he looked much younger. Now he had passed a few days of pleasure with Ann, he felt guilty, he had gone off task. The more he thought, the worse his guilt became, it was Sunday the 22nd – he would make a start tonight.

CHAPTER 55

JACK HAD ALTERNATED BETWEEN STANDING and sitting through the whole 2 hours of singing, clapping and wailing; the whole time trying to think how he would confront Bernard. Now as the pantomime was nearing the end, he was still no nearer a solution. The congregation was now being urged to come up and be saved, people were forming queues to move up to the dais, and then the idea came to Jack in a flash. Bernard was beside Algernon as he blessed each person kneeling at the edge of the stage. There were so many people milling around the stage that perhaps he could speak to Bernard unexpectedly.

It took a long time before Jack came to the dais but finally he was there, on his knees with his head bowed, waiting his turn to be saved. Algernon placed a hand on his head and said, "Bless you, in the name of Jesus Lord of Light." then moved onto the next head.

As Bernard drew level with Jack, Jack stood up a mere 9" away, and stared into his face. "Why did you kill her?" he asked quietly looking directly into Bernard's eyes. The shock was devastating, he could see from the Bernard's facial expression that it had taken him completely off balance.

Bernard opened his mouth in shock and horror. "I didn't mean to, I didn't mean to – I..." he reeled backwards, stumbling he ran from the dais. Jack turned calmly and mingled with the others as if nothing had happened. There was so much going on, so many people jostling to get back to their seats, others still trying to make their way to the dais and it was all over in seconds. Algernon looked around as Bernard ran from the stage but carried on blessing his flock.

As Jack left the marquee and returned to his car, he knew, beyond all doubt, that Bernard had killed his little girl.

CHAPTER 56

Fᴿᴼᴹ ᴀ ᴄʜᴇᴍɪsᴛ, Jᴀᴄᴋ ʙᴏᴜɢʜᴛ 3 different types of headache tables and a bottle of cough mixture. Using his official chemist ID card, he also purchased a disposable hypodermic syringe.

The taxi driver picked him up outside the post office. "Where can I get a line of smack?" Jack asked.

He turned and eyed Jack cautiously, "You on the level man?" he said.

"Yes," said Jack, "and there's $20 in it for you."

He continued to stare at Jack for a moment, then "OK, sit tight." as he drove for a short distance, pulling up outside a block of flats. Winding down the window, he whistled to a youth sitting on a low wall in front of the building. "It'll cost you a $20," he told Jack, "for the good stuff." Jack passed him 2 x $20 as the youth approached the car. He turned to the youth, now standing at his window, "Gimmie two barrels." he said holding out one of the $20 notes.

The youth went to take the note and pass him a piece of silver paper. "Good stuff," he said, "I don't want no shit man."

The young lad took the $20 and handed over the package. "You wouldn't know shit from clay old man." he laughed, making his way back to sit on the wall. The driver snorted and drove away, passing the silver paper back to Jack. He opened it and inside was a small quantity of white powder.

Back in his room, Jack took 3 tablets from one bottle, 2 from another and 4 from the last. Placing them in a small steel bowl he had brought with him, he ground them into a fine powder. Taking a small measure from a leather pouch, he placed a quantity of the cough medicine into the powder and mixed it to a paste. He filled the bowl with water and placed it on the cooker hot plate. This, he allowed to boil until all the water had evaporated, leaving a red/grey deposit in the bowl. Finally he added the heroin to the mix and spent considerable time mixing the two thoroughly together. Once this was done, he added surgical spirit until he had sufficient to fill the syringe, which he did and placed in his jacket pocket in a tobacco pouch.

At 7:15pm, Jack parked his car in the car park. As he walked with the crowds towards the entrance he noticed, standing just inside the lobby, Bernard was inspecting the people as they entered. To his right stood two men in grey suits, hair cropped, tall, muscular men impeccably dressed, upper class expensive muscle. Jack froze for a moment then turned, as if forgetting something, and returned to his car. He sat there watching until most of the people had entered the marquee, the car park was empty, and Bernard and the two men followed the others in. This had thrown him off course again, he had to think hard. He had no choice, he had to go in.

Jack left his car and walked toward the marquee listening to the singing coming from inside. He went to the left of the entrance, down the side of the marquee. Inside the speakers boomed, Algernon was in full stride describing Bernard prior to his enlightenment. As he reached the area level with the dais he could see that a flap in the side had been laced up. Through this he could see into the marquee with clear vision to the stage. So close, Bernard was standing about 6' away shifting uneasily from one foot to the other. If only he could get closer. Realising he could not get to him from there, Jack retraced his steps along the side of the marquee. About half way along, the sides were loose and a gap of about 6" was showing between the grass and the bottom of the side sheets. Waiting until the congregation rose to sing 'Marching with the Lord', he dropped to the ground, lying full length on the grass, then rolled under and stood quickly. Nobody seemed to notice.

In the tobacco pouch, safely tucked into Jack's pocket, was a large dose of heroin, enough to kill. However, the subtle difference between this and any ordinary overdose was that the other drugs that Jack had mixed with the heroin would prevent any medical intervention to purge the drug before it had served its purpose. Once into the system, there was no way out. Injected intramuscularly it would take about an hour and fifteen minutes to take effect, death was sure and certain within 24 hours. Even with the power and money of the Godleman camp to get urgent medical attention, should they suspect Bernard of any overdosing, it would be useless. The household drugs would surely be detected at a post mortem, but their deadly purpose would not be recognised.

Jack carefully positioned himself after the blessing in the centre, near the rear door, in a position he knew that Algernon and Bernard would have to pass to reach the lobby – as they did on the first night. With great care, he undid the zip on the tobacco pouch and took out the syringe inside his pocket. He could feel the surge of adrenalin and his heart pounded, a primitive feeling came over him and he could feel the hairs down his spine rise.

The wailing, chanting and whole razzmatazz had started; Algernon placed his arms around Bernard and started the journey to the entrance. With all the pushing and jostling Jack was afraid he may stick someone else with the needle as the pair slowly advanced. They were passing Jack now and a large man with a florid face and ginger beard had leaned over Jack and slapped Bernard on the shoulder violently, "Well done Brother," he shouted "Hallelujah!" Jack took this opportunity to lean in and punch the syringe hard into Bernard's left buttock, punching the plunger completely down, the whole syringe emptied into him. At the same instant, Bernard's sharp cry was stifled by a woman who threw her arms around his neck and screamed, "Praise to the Lord for your salvation."

As the crowd surged around them, Jack escaped between a gap that had opened up leading to the entrance. He slipped into the lobby and was soon outside. Forcing himself not to run, he walked until he reached his car, started the engine and drove away. He could still hear the Hosanna's ringing out from the marquee.

The Manse had been completely redecorated especially for its revered guests. Algernon strode through the double mahogany doors onto the polished teak block floor of the hall. "My god I feel good, did you see the collection tonight my pigeon,"

he said to Bernard, "over $5000. Wahoo the Lord is good to his humble servants."

An elderly man with grey hair entered the hall from another passage on the right. "Anything you require sir?" he enquired.

"No Jenkins, I believe I have what I require with me thank you, you may retire. Please wake me at 8:30am with coffee."

"Yes sir, Goodnight." The old man turned and walked down the passage he came from.

Algernon pushed open the double doors into a large lounge, furnished with the American Colonel Style furniture, and walked over to a drinks tray. Taking two heavy crystal glasses, he poured a stiff Chivas Regal into each and held one out to Bernard. "Here we are my pigeon." he said, "I think we'll have it on the couch tonight, I feel like being young again."

"My arse hurts like hell." said Bernard rubbing his left buttock.

"Oh dear, that means I'll have to use more Vaseline I suppose."

"No, not my asshole, my arse." Bernard said as he started to sway, beads of sweat stood out on his forehead and top lip. He dropped the glass, which bounced on the wooden floor, splashing whisky on the Persian Rug. He swayed again the pitched full length on his face.

Algernon called for the doctor who immediately called for an ambulance, which he and Algernon then followed to the hospital.

The doctor in casualty examined the chalk white Bernard, "Well," he spoke to Algernon's personal doctor, 'without a detailed examination, I would say that he's taken an overdose."

"That was my exact diagnosis." Replied the doctor.

"OK, put him into the detoxification program." he said to the nurse. "Pump him out." Turning to Algernon, "You'd better come back tomorrow, there's nothing you can do now."

Algernon arrived back at the hospital at 8:00am to be advised that Bernard had died. "I'm afraid that he died during the night, we were unable to clean up his system of the massive dose of heroin."

Algernon was visibly shocked. "That's not possible, how did he get it? Why, I don't understand."

"We have examined him thoroughly but until a post mortem has been carried out I can't comment any further. He must have taken it orally as we can't find marks on his legs or arms which are the normal places they inject."

"They, they," Algernon questioned, "what do you mean, they?"

"I'm sorry, but you don't normally take a massive dose of heroin as a trail run for your first time." He did however start to ramble a bit before he died, I wrote down what I could understand, I suppose I should hand it to the police but as it's obviously just rambling, I'll let you have it." He handed Algernon a piece of paper.

> *He found me........Belinda......... I didn't mean to.........I saw her on his motorbike – walking..... bitch........bitch, wouldn't let me........in the arse......in the arse...........how did she know...........she couldn't know...............he knew!*

CHAPTER 57

Fifty-three competitors stood in the early morning on the red bare earth. The rules had been carefully explained to Clyde the previous day. A full 50 mile course in the mountain foothills. Covering the entire course at intervals were brightly coloured woven rings hanging on threads. The winner was the first one back with one of each of the colours; red, yellow, green, blue, white and black. Each competitor carried a wooden spear, upon which he had to collect the 6 rings. The rings had been suspended early that morning so it was impossible to bypass any of the set course. Only those competitors who arrived at the finish before the sun dipped behind Alkhramhamip, the largest of the range of mountains to the west of the arena, would be awarded points. It was a gruelling race covering very difficult terrain; 90% of the entrants had competed before but only 6 had ever completed it in the time allowed.

Slowly the glow in the sky increased as the yellow orb, the very rim of the sun, showed over the flat desert to the east. The flag dropped, the race had begun. The horses were corralled in the stockade to one side of the arena, each competitor had to race to the stockade and find his mount. The horses were all saddled the same, a small Arab saddle, short reigns and snaffle bit. Fifty-three horses, all loose in a 10m square fenced stockade. It had taken several hours before the last rider had even mounted his horse the previous year as the first man out, having opened the pole gate rode off shouting and shrieking, driving the majority of other horses out into the arena where a desperate melee of men and horses had resulted in chaos.

As the flag dropped the men started running to the stockade but Clyde stood still. Adel watched, holding her breath, why was he not moving? Behind the post and rail fence of the stockade, she could see the shiny black filly, flaring her wide nostrils and prancing in anticipation. Then the filly stood ears to the front, she had heard the man, the guttural sounds of the ancient language and she knew what to do. Breaking into a run, she went straight for the rails and gathering her long legs she took it in one high leap and cantered towards the man standing waiting. For a moment the whole scene ran into slow motion, the crowd rose in appreciation. As the beautiful black animal reached the man she stopped and stood at the ready. Clyde took two steps and lightly vaulted onto her back, he patted the sleek neck, gathered the reigns and they left the arena; the race was on.

The first part of the course ran flat towards the foothills. Just into the tree line the red markers fluttered in the hot breeze. Knowing that the gruelling course would tax both him and the horse to the limit, Clyde rode without pushing and the black filly rode at a steady pace. He took for granted the way the Arab horse responded to him, without question. A bond between them, in such a short time, was truly amazing.

Gradually the track became more difficult, large loose stones replaced the sand and gravel as it started to rise. As he reached the first rise, Clyde could see the red markers. Beneath the trees to his right, hanging from the tree were the white tokens. Clyde rode up, placing the short spear through the nearest, the thin thread broke easily. As Clyde continued his steady climb, other competitors riding hard, started to overhaul his early lead. The first to pass him was a hard young Arab with his black hair tied up in a pony tail, riding a large brown stallion. Already his horse was flecked with sweat, its eyes wild as they galloped past. As the stallion caught the filly's scent it took all the Arabs strength to keep his mount from slowing. Clattering, slipping and sliding, the pair disappeared around the bend in the track. By midday 10 riders had overtaken Clyde; of these Clyde had now passed three.

The big brown stallion lay on its side, its foreleg smashed, the white bone splintered and stuck out of the mangled leg. Clyde reigned up and dismounted his horse. "You are not expected to help Infidel." the Arab explained, "Go." He lay on the horse's neck as it struggled to rise. He looked back at Clyde. "My first chance at the competition and my father's best horse, what am I to do?" Clyde from the horse to the rider, he no longer looked hard, just a youth in his late teens. He could see in his eyes the horse's pain and discomfort. Inexperience and youthful exuberance had finished this horse.

Clyde carried a boot knife, a slim razor sharp blade with a white bone handle, in a soft leather sheath tucked into his calf length boots. He drew the knife and looked to the youth who hung his head and nodded slightly. Clyde reached down to the sleek muscled neck and felt the inch thick jugular pumping blood to the brain, near the surface just below the horse's jaw. Without hesitation he firmly drew the blade across and down through the skin and muscle and across the blue green wall of the pulsing pipe. It was severed in one forceful glance. The bright red blood sprayed in a sold jet as the heart pumped against the released pressure. It was all over in seconds, the horse relaxed as the blood supply to the brain ceased. Clyde could do no more and he left the boy and the dead horse. As he mounted his hose the boy stood, "Thank you," he said simply, "Good work."

Clyde raised his arm in acknowledgement as he rode away.

High now in the mountains Clyde had 4 of the 6 tokens. The track continued up between the large boulders and Clyde dismounted and led his horse on foot. Dark Side of the Moon licked his neck beneath the hat, Clyde patted her neck. He took two glucose tablets from the pouch on his belt and popped them in his mouth; they fizzed slightly, orange in taste. At the top of the rocky track, Clyde looked back and out to the east, the blue sky stretched in a huge umbrella covering the undulating desert. The thin green ribbon of the river and its attendant green growth slowly petered out in the middle distance. Below him he could see the town and the arena, the flags a tiny splash of coloured movement. In front of him, to the west, a flat plateau of sandy rock and bushes preceded the rise of the great black mountains of Africa, forbidding and majestic peak upon peak into the hazy distance. As he approached the markers the horse snorted and became uneasy. The markers were attached to rusty iron rings hanging off the rock face, a smooth bowl near the edge of the plateau; with a protective rock face about 15' high. As they approached the horse became more and more uneasy. Clyde too was feeling uncomfortable; the hairs on his arms stood up and a prickle of dread ran down his back. He looked at the horse, she mouthed the bit and cantered, picking up her feet and snorting. Was she imparting something to him or could he feel it also? Along the rock face there were hundreds of the rusty rings, the chain links hammered around iron bars driven into the rock face. Some of the rings were so corroded that they had almost disappeared in the red orange cancer of rust. As the cool mountain wind swept round the rock face, it moaned and the iron chains rattled against the rock.

Suddenly he recalled Assam's conversation of his ancestors raiding beyond the mountains and bringing back line of blacks chained together. 'Slaves', the place was undeniably evil. The horse was behaving so badly it was taking all of Clyde's power to restrain it. He himself had never experienced such a tangible evil; an ancient sin long since past but somehow retained in the rock. There was a stench of faeces and fear. Could he imagine such a strong smell, like a huge dead beast in the last stages of petrifaction? He snatched a red token from the 6 hanging from a rusty metal bar and quickly mounted. The horse, pleased to be going, cantered rapidly down the track away from the old slave pen.

The downhill track was even more dangerous than the uphill. The road shifted beneath them and rocks twisted under the horse's feet. Clyde knew well enough to dismount or he would end up with a lame horse, or worse.

It was well into the afternoon when Clyde approached the last markers. During the whole day he had seen only a handful of competitors and the only contact he had made with any of them was the boy with the horse whom he had stopped to help. As he neared, he could see 3 or 4 horses. The markers were hung from a large Acacia tree. Clyde could see the threads where the last tokens had been; the black ones, but they were not there. Carefully he slid off the horse's back and stood facing the men. "Well done Infidel." one of the men said as he stood forward of the others. "You have done well to get this far. Do you have the other 5 tokens?" Looking at Clyde's spear he could clearly see that he did. "We have decided that an Arab will win today." the man continued. "This is as far as you will go."

Clyde studied the Arab carefully. He wore calf length boots with 3 buckled straps over thick muscular legs, black shorts and a green tee-shirt with the sleeves cut short showing heavy arms. His pock marked face had a long scar down one side which pulled his face into a grin. Unusually, his black hair was short cropped; his eyes were a light green-brown, muddy coloured white blood was the background; he was a dangerous looking man. He carried a riot police fighting stick, a black rod with a short peg sticking out at right angles, used properly a very effective weapon.

"Now give me the tokens and keep your body whole. If you do not, you will never be the same." the man giggled, obviously this excited him. As he approached, Clyde bent his knees slightly and the hair rose on this neck, his eyes glowed eerily green. The man kept coming but he had stopped giggling and was now more cautious. Slowly Clyde placed the spear on the ground and past over it, the man now only a few feet away. Without warning he jabbed at Clyde with the riot stick, hard and violently. As the stick came forward Clyde side stepped slightly, grabbed the stick and pulled on it. The move surprised the man as he had expected his aggression to unnerve Clyde. He was already slightly off balance as Clyde's elbow hit him below the arm holding the stick. For a moment he was completely numb, but he moved fast to recover; he wasn't quick enough, Clyde was now behind him. He kicked his right leg out from under him and the man fell to the floor. Clyde stood on his hand and kicked again, this time at his elbow, the arm broke with a snap. The speed and ferocity of Clyde's attack on a very powerful opponent had unnerved the other three men.

Now, one of the others was rushing forward, also holding a riot stick. He struck Clyde on his left shoulder as Clyde simultaneously landed his right elbow on the man' jaw, breaking it. The man's mouth hung open as he shrieked in pain, his jawbone snapped in two places and teeth showing through his split cheek. Clyde straightened and massaged his shoulder where he had been hit, nothing broken. The man sank to his knees, holding his shattered jaw, the blood running through his fingers from his split cheek and disappearing into the dry earth. Clyde walked towards the remaining men who immediately mounted their horses and rode off. He returned and collected his spear, with the 5 tokens, grabbing the reigns he mounted. His shoulder began to ache, it had been an exhausting day, and the adrenalin had burnt up a lot of his energy.

He estimated he had two hours left before the time ran out but he was still a long way from the arena. Dark Side of the Moon was also tiring, rock strewn paths and gullies take a lot out of a horse. Picking a way through it is hard and she slipped and slithered a good deal. A short branch had nicked her hind quarters and the blood from the wound smeared her glossy haunch. Sweat covered her front withers like a grey scum. Then a rock turned under her front left hoof and she fell. As she did, Clyde managed to get his leg clear of her body and rolled away. He encouraged her to rise. She stood with difficulty, favouring the sprained leg. "OK, come on girl, we'll trot together." Holding her reigns as support, they started. The horse found it easier without a rider and shuffled on limping badly.

An hour later they came to a level patch and stopped. The river broke surface here in the rocks and Clyde led the horse into the cold water, standing her up to her knees in the clear mountain water.

The last leg was far worse that the SAS course on Salisbury Plains. His breath caught painfully in his throat, his knees and ankles ached and the shoulder struck by the Arab burned and throbbed. The horse helped immensely though, taking a lot of the strain, they ran together. They cleared the trees and the arena was now half a mile across the sandy plain. The sun was almost touching the tall black peak. "Come on girl, come on." he breathed as they picked up speed and covering the distance easily. The horse knew and her drumming hoof beat became a tempo. Clyde's own feet now touched the ground one in three as he clung to the reigns. They entered the arena as the last rays spread across the yellow sand.

Clyde and Dark Side of the Moon had been the fifth competitor to arrive back at the arena. 2 had all 6 tokens, 3 others including Clyde had 5. They were separated by time and awarded points accordingly. Clyde was awarded 10 points.

CHAPTER 58

CLYDE WOKE AND STRETCHED, HE felt surprisingly good considering yesterday. He lay on the silken sheets for a moment, he could see again her appreciation and delight and a warm churning sensation in his stomach. He jumped up from the mound of pillows, pulling on shorts he went through a series of warm up exercises. Just as the sweat began to bead on his forehead Assam came through the tent opening. "Good, good." he said approvingly. "You have another long day ahead."

At mid afternoon Clyde was in the semi-finals. The fighting, he had found out earlier, was never the same. It depended on the opponent. In the main part, it was wrestling. To win a contestant had to hold down flat both shoulders of his opponent for 5 seconds; however the rules were not that simple. In addition to holding your opponent for 5 seconds to win, how you got him to this position was vital. There were no rules as to how you did this but if your opponent was incapable – by being unconscious or shocked of resisting you – neither one of you scored any points.

Clyde was facing the tall, almost black Arab, his long hair tied in a ponytail. His eyes were close together and he had a cast in one eye. He was taller than Clyde with narrow hips and heavy shoulders. They faced each other and bowed slightly. As they straightened the man kicked out with his right foot, fast as a striking snake, Clyde twisted slightly to the left, the blow was meant for his balls, but the foot struck him on his right thigh. It struck with considerable force, causing a numbing pain, and for a few seconds he had to favour the leg. Wearily he faced the man, a sly grin spread over the Arabs face; he could see the blow had hurt Clyde. Lightly he dropped to the ground on his behind and swept his legs to take Clyde behind the knee but Clyde jumped and the man's legs swept passed without connecting. Clyde placed his foot on the man's hand and kicked him under the arm. He pulled out his hand and rolled away, getting to his feet they faced each other. The Arab jabbed a right hand punch. Clyde swayed to the left, grabbed the arm, placed his arm on the elbow and forced the man to the ground. Holding the arm he dropped to the ground and placed his other leg over the man's shoulder, slowly the two shoulders were pressed into the dust. The crowd roared 1, 2, 3, 4, 5 – Clyde was through to the final.

Clyde had seen Ramool exercising before the contest, his long black hair tied tight in a bun at the back of his head. Now as he faced him the head shone like a polished billiard ball, smooth and freshly shaven. As they approached each other Clyde took in the barrel chest, the well shaped muscular legs and between his massive shoulders his neck bulging with muscle. He looked directly at Clyde; he was the only competitor who had held Clyde's green eyes. His face broke into a big grin with large white teeth; it was an open honest smile.

"Al akra Infidel (good luck)." he said. "And you." replied Clyde.

They bowed slightly, standing apart Ramool offered Clyde an outstretched open fingered hand, an invitation. Clyde placed his palm against it and locked fingers, the Arab's hand was dry, slowly the fingers closed. He was a good 6" shorter than Clyde and as he exerted pressure to his hand, the biceps in his right arm bunched. The power in this man's arm was awesome, Clyde had to bend his knees to come down to his height, and slowly Ramool forced him to his knees. Realizing the strength of this man, Clyde decided that he would have to use agility to have any chance. Placing his free hand on the bald dome head he vaulted over, still holding Ramool's hand. Even with his strength Ramool had to go with Clyde or the wrist would break, he whipped over, and they broke their grip. Ramool landed like a cat on his feet and whirled round to meet Clyde, but Clyde was too quick for him. As he turned Clyde side stepped, caught him by the leg and pulled. Ramool fell on his back. Quickly Clyde fell beside him, placed an arm over his neck, caught him by the other arm from behind and completed a full neck lock. Ramool pulled first one of his own legs under him and then the other slowly pulling himself up and taking Clyde with him. They stood, Ramool hunched over with Clyde applying a full neck lock from behind, Clyde's hands firmly locked around Ramool thick neck. Ramool sucked in his breath, expanded his chest and exerted pressure with his arms. By now Clyde was beginning to realise that the man he was fighting had an agility to match his own and a strength which he could not match. Slowly Ramool brought down his arms and broke Clyde's lock. Clyde bent and grabbed an arm as he released, bending it against the joint; as he did he exposed his own ribs. Mentally he cursed, all Ramool had to do was a short jab and Clyde could not protect or counter, the blow did not come. For half an hour they parried and wrestled with nei- ther gaining any real advantage. Ramool made no attempt to strike Clyde by kicking or punching, he just used strength and agility. Both men were now slick with sweat as Clyde manoeuvred Ramool into a position with his legs locked behind each other and a sleeper hold on his neck. Slowly, unbelievably, the massive shoulders moved to the floor as Ramool seemed to relax both shoulders – 1, 2 and then like a steel spring, his muscular body straightened. He locked a hard, steel like arm over Clyde's shoulders. As Clyde released his locked legs slowly, Ramool pulled one arm round, then the other and held them together; tipping his body Clyde slid slowly down onto the back of his neck and felt his shoulders touch the dusty earth. He wriggled but could not stop the force pushing him into the ground. 1, 2, 3, desper- ately he tried to move, 4, the crowd were silent – 5. Clyde had lost, Ramool released him and stood up holding Clyde's hand and pulling him with him. The crowd started to roar. Still holding Clyde's arm he held up his hand. "Al behr helkr an Tehar (Pass me a knife)," he shouted. An Arabic dagger landed beside him. He drew the edge of the blade across his palm and a thin line of blood followed the blade. Taking Clyde's hand he gently drew the edge across his palm. Joining hands, he embraced Clyde before drawing apart. Ramool held up his hand and the crowd went quiet, waiting expectantly.

"You all know me." he said in Arabic. "I am Ramool. I have won this second day in the great competition every year since my eighteenth year of age. I am now 27. In all those 9 years of competition I have never fought a better man. My only regret is that I may have spoiled this mans chances to win the greatest prize of all, to win this competition complete. This man is now my brother and I salute his courage and skills as a fighting man." The crowd went wild.

CHAPTER 59

THE THIRD AND FINAL DAY of competition had arrived. Clyde now had 25 points having been awarded 15 points for his second day of competition. Ramool had 25 points also, having scored no points on the fist day. Achmed and Ramhal had scored 25 each for the first day and Cahlede had scored nothing on the first day by had picked up 5 points on the second. Clyde was among the leaders.

The bow competition was divided into 3 different events. The first was standard concentric rings with a bull's eye 4" in diameter in the centre. The competitors would shoot from 150 yards, each allowed 3 arrows. The last arrow only would count unless they elected to stop at either the first or the second attempt. If they shot a poor arrow for the third attempt it made no difference, it was the third one that scored any points.

Calhede's bow was an exact twin to the one Clyde had come across in the Arab store. Together they assembled the competition bows, Ancient weapons born in a different age yet still capable, in skilled hands, of great feats of skill and accuracy.

At 150 paces, the 12" diameter targets looked very small! A total of 150 bowmen assembled in the arena, each holding there arrows. Clyde stood amongst the competitors and waited for his turn at one of the 10 target places set. Only the top 25 scores would go through to the next round.

His number was called and Clyde approached the number 3 stand and selected three arrows, these he stuck in the red earth in front of him. Taking a deep breath he placed the wooden arrow in the bow, the yellow feathers contrasting with the black painted shaft. The distance was 150 yards, a very long shot indeed. Carefully and deliberately he pulled back the string, taking up the considerable tension with his right arm, the forearm muscle bunched under the load. The old bow maker's craft had placed a pull strength of 120lbs in the fully drawn bow and as the string touched Clyde's lips, the poundage was exact. Clyde released the string and the old bow imparted that energy to the arrow. In a parabolic curve the black shaft arched over the 150 yards and buried half its length into the sand bags behind the target, leaving the yellow flight feathers 4" above the black circle. Clyde carefully took the red tipped arrow and recalculated his shot allowing a smaller drop of the arrow. The black shaft cut the top half of the target midway between the bull and the outer edge. This arrow was the 92nd to be released and the first to cut the target. A loud roar went up from the watching crowd, over the last 2 days, Clyde had become extremely popular. "Let it stand." he said as he walked away.

Calhede's third arrow struck the black ring at one side. They were both through to the next section. This was quickly set up while lunch, prepared by the many Arab women, was passed around and eaten casually either standing or squatting on the ground. Many different meats in sauces, together with a flat pancake type of bread rolled into a kebab. None of the bowman attempted to drink the potent palm wine.

The crowd was aware that the man with the green eyes known as the Infidel now had a good chance of winning the overall competition. The second section would still not decide a winner; one of the other bowmen had scored a complete black, a central arrow, and had also done well in the horse section.

The next bowman ship test carried points. The large round targets were erected at a distance of 75 yards this time and were divided into 3 segments of green, blue and red. Close to the centre where each segment touched scored 10 points and this amount decreased as it neared the outer edge. The points were scored by these amounts;

however the sequence had to be green first, then blue and finally red. If an arrow hit the target out of sequence that amount was deducted from the competitors score.

Clyde's first arrow struck the outer edge of the green segment, 1 point scored. His next cut the target a the 5 point mark but just inside the red ring - 5 points away from his total. His total score was now 21 points with one arrow left. Slowly he locked the bright red feathers into the string of his bow. The centre ring was just 3" in diameter giving a target less than 2 wide and 1 ½ long wedge shaped. The last section, Clyde knew, was a one arrow hit or miss. This one will decide his win or lose. As the arrow reached his cheek his breath slightly ruffled the feathers. For a moment, the string vibrated slightly with the tension across the brass bands bound around the laminated limb. Concentrating hard, his vision clear, Clyde could see the target and focused on the wedge shaped section coloured red. The arrow struck exactly where it was aimed, leaving the red feathers still trembling, and the matching colour of the feathers made it impossible to see against the red background. An examiner confirmed top score by raising a lollipop like stick from the target. The maximum 10 points scored.

At the end of the second section Calhede and Achmed were equal with 30 points each. Clyde led with 31 points. Now for Clyde to win he had one last task; a simple line drawn in the sand 600 yards away; the Archers stood. To win this great competition an arrow had to pass over the line 600 yards away. It was an almost impossible distance for a long bow. In all the years of the games, only two arrows had ever landed over the line.

Using one of the original arrows he had obtained with the bow, Clyde took a deep breath and released the ancient arrow. Of the 9 he had, three were speed arrows; light and thinner than the hunting ones. The old shaft seemed to quiver as it sped to the top of its arch. As it hit the sand, just 3 inches over the line, it splintered and the shaft shattered. Years of being stored in the goat skin quiver had weakened the old wooden shaft. For a full second the silence was deafening before the roar of approval. Clyde was indeed a popular winner.

Achmed, Calhede and Ramool carried Clyde shoulder high above the crowd; everyone was reaching to touch him to signify their approval. The great competition was over for another 5 years and they would tell many a story of the Infidel's feat.

A great feast was prepared for the end of the competition. However, the massive overdose of adrenalin had drained Clyde and he found it difficult to relax and enjoy the atmosphere. Similarly, Adel caught Clyde's mood and was content to sit beside him in almost silence. He shivered as a small chill wind blew in from the river. Somehow it carried with it an illusive foreboding. The competition had taken his mind off the previous months; this small change caused by the wind brought it back. It's finished now he thought, Vanessa's killer wiped off the earth in an instant. But if felt wrong, he knew every single one of those killed in the explosion were better away from society permanently, but the feeling persisted.

That night he and Adel crept away and lay together on the scented rugs, holding each other closely. In the morning, the ashes of the celebrations still warm, Clyde walked slowly to the river. He stood on the gravel bank overlooking the green water. The sun came as a golden orb clearing the red sand to the east striking the black mountains guarding Africa, brooding, solid a barrier to the red sands of Arabia. A small plane flew out of the sun; its engine note altered as the pilot throttled off and dropped the plane onto the runway beside the arena. It seemed somehow the pilot carried news which would alter whatever future plans he was making.

Assam ran to meet the pilot, his baggy trousers tucked into his boots. Clyde walked towards the plane but although he could hear the voices he was too far away to make out what they were saying. The pilot and Assam turned toward him as Assam pointed towards him; Clyde knew his instinct had not failed him. As he approached, more people came to join the pilot and Assam, all taking in Arabic.

"Clyde, this is Hanic Dunbar, our chief of disruptive services and a damned good pilot." Clyde stepped up and took the young man's offered hand, it was slim and strong. "He brings bad news I am afraid." said Assam. "Apparently the man you sought to destroy was not harmed, and he alone escaped the blast. However Infidel, you wiped out the entire hornets nest, a clean kill apart from your 'Wolf', he indeed leads a charmed life.

Clyde made immediate plans to leave with the pilot.

Later that day he held Adel's face between his hands and looked into her dark eyes as they slowly filled with tears. A fat drop formed at the corner and ran down her cheek, then another, then another. "Will you come for me when it's over?" she said in a broken voice.

"Will you be waiting?" he asked.

"Yes, definitely yes." she said softly.

"You know I must go, don't you?" he asked. She nodded gently. He kissed her lips; a light lingering soft kiss and then he was gone.

CHAPTER 60

MARY KNOCKED ON THE BRIGHT red door with the brass knocker. "Mrs. Barber? she questioned as the door was opened.

"Yes." the lady replied.

"May I talk to you for a minute?" Mary asked "It's about Terry." Fear filled the old lady's face and she became uncertain.

"Please," pushed Mary "it's very important.

"He's in the hospital." the old lady said in a halting voice.

"I know. I'm a nurse from the hospital." replied Mary showing her staff nurse badge.

"Come in." she said at last standing to one side to let Mary pass. Hesitatingly she looked up and down the deserted street before closing the door. She showed Mary into the small lounge. "Would you like a cup of tea?"

"Yes please." said Mary hoping this would relieve some of the tension. When Mrs. Barber came back into the room, Mary decided to jump in with both feet. "Mrs. Barber, I know about the beating, loosing your tooth; I know everything."

Mrs. Barber dropped the tray with a crash, and sunk to the carpet among the debris, covering up her face with her hands she started to cry. Mary rushed to her side, the thin shoulders shook uncontrollably. Putting her arm around her, Mary helped her into a chair.

"If he finds out that anybody knows, he'll kill me!" she cried. "I know he will."

"He won't find out," Mary said, "I promise." Slowly Mrs. Barber raised her eyes to meet Mary. "He did it to make you lie for him, didn't he?" Mrs. Barber nodded.

"You told the police he was in his room all night when they came to question him?" Again she nodded. Mary felt a great wave of satisfaction now she had convinced herself that he was guilty, and she had worked out exactly how to extract vengeance.

Mary knelt on the carpet before Mrs. Barber and took her hands in her own, "He won't ever find out that we have talked. And I promise he will never beat you again. He is going to be in hospital for a while yet, before he comes out perhaps you should go away for a holiday. Have you anywhere you could go that he does not know about?"

She thought for a moment, wiping her eyes with the hanky Mary had given her. "I have a friend in Wales with a cottage in the hills near Caernarvon. I'm sure she would be delighted if I went to stay with her for a while." Mary, satisfied, stood and cleared up the mess from the accident.

As she was headed for the door Mary turned to Mrs. Barber, "You make those arrangements to go away, don't tell anyone, and I'll let you know when he is due out of hospital." She took hold of the old lady's shoulders, kissed her gently on the cheek and left.

As she drove away she carefully went through her plans. Given the information she had just learnt, she knew that the police could never get Mrs. Barber to admit to lying to cover for her nephew. Yet without this information, they wouldn't have the break necessary to make a case against him. She stuffed all qualms to the back of her mind about what she planned to do; justifying it with the thought of her daughter lying in the cold earth and Mrs. Barber, a terrified old lady, beaten senseless by an oaf who was not fit to remain in society. In her eyes he had forfeited all right to forgiveness and mercy.

CHAPTER 61

MARY ENTERED THE SMALL WARD, Terry Anderson lay on the bed propped up with pillows, his head completely swathed in bandages except for his eyes nose and mouth. Two small capillary tubes came from beneath the bandages and fed into a complicated electronic machine. The green screen flickered as a line pulsed across it, peaking and troughing constantly, his eyes were closed when she entered. What a pity she thought, if this was a life support machine she could just switch it off and be rid of this monster. The scan was only monitoring brain impulses to assess damage; so far there was no evidence of any. Suddenly the eyes opened and looked at Mary; she stared back at the grey green eyes, it was as if he knew that she knew of his dreadful deed and was mocking her. She turned on her heel and left the room.

Tex recovered rapidly; within 3 weeks he was off all forms of medication. The surgeon removed the stitches in his head, remarking how rapidly he had healed. Tex steadfastly refused to make any statement regarding the night of the fight. After 4 weeks, the shaved head had grown a black covering of hair, hiding the scars where the surgeon had grafted the bone and patched the badly smashed skull.

From what Arthur had told her about Tex, Mary had pieced together his psychopathic illness. Arthur had told her that Tex could only reach a sexual climax while having pain inflicted on him. He had told Mary that his sister had had to stick pins into his thighs to give him an erection. The situation was getting worse; with a higher level of pain having to be given. His phobia was that it is very difficult to find girls prepared to carry out this sort of perversion. Physologically a complete reversal of violent sex crimes, normally the pain has to be inflicted on others by the person to get sexual gratification, a self debilitating and physcological destructive state for a man of Tex's make up.

Mary placed the thermometer in his mouth, she had not spoken a word to him, he lay arrogantly sprawled on the bed, the hospital pyjamas open exposing his chest and lower body. The bandages had been removed but the wound was still covered with a dressing, he had been there for 4 weeks.). Steeling herself Mary placed her hand on his chest and with her nail drew a line down between his pictorial muscles, she saw his jawbone tighten and his stomach muscles rippled. She heard a slight hiss as he drew in breath, 4 weeks without release was his limit, "Harder." he whispered. Mary pressed until the nail cut into his skin, slowly she saw his erection rise and push out the front of his pyjamas. Suddenly she withdrew her hand and took out the thermometer; quickly she left the room, sickened but now she knew the truth.

CHAPTER 62

MARY KNEW SHE WAS EMBARKING on a dangerous journey, she had to be extremely carefully and fully aware. How could she get this sick dog of a person to trust her enough to get him vulnerable and on his own? Vulnerable was going to the easy part; having a vast knowledge of drugs, and although difficult, she could get small quantities without risk. Rohypnol, the date rape drug, was going to be fervourent. Getting him to trust her and being able to get him on his own was going to require some more thought. However, the answer to this came easier than she had imagined.

Even though Mary was desperate to avenge her daughter's death convinced that Terry killed her, she could not bring herself to enter any kind of intimate relationship with him even though he made it clear he wanted her to pay him attention.

CHAPTER 63

I T WAS WELL KNOWN IN town that 'The Dragon' was a Bikie pub where the Satan's Disciples regularly met on Friday nights in the Animal bar. The pub was located in a rural area just outside of town. Although the landlord was not entirely happy about the situation, they spent well and kept the violence down to an almost acceptable level so, he tolerated them for now; he would live to regret this. How though could Mary use this to carry out her plan? She wasn't too concerned about the Rohypnol being detected in his body as it was unlikely that a drug test would be carried out on a dead bikie, but how to administer it?

Mary was sure that if she turned up on a Friday night Tex would, by his very nature, not think it strange but consider it his irresistible charm and magnetism that drew her in; to drug him would be easy. How to get him out into the car park without incriminating herself could prove a little more difficult.

The following Friday night around 10:30pm Mary parked her car opposite The Dragon and waited until it closed. Just after 11:00pm, the car park deserted except for a half dozen or so motorbikes, the doors opened and 6 or 7 bikers came out laughing, shouting and stumbling their way to their parked motorbikes. Tax was the last one out and with him was the same young girl Mary had seen him with at the hot dog van.

The other bikers roared off toward town leaving Tex and the girl on their own in the car park. She lifted her short skirt, sat herself on the motorbike seat and raised her knees high placing her feet on the seat. Without hesitation Tex undid his pants and proceeded to have sex with her on the bike. In that moment Mary knew how she would accomplish her plan. One Friday night soon she would be that girl, but not for sex.

She waited for them to finish and ride away and then waited some more. The pub lights went out and a lounge light went on in the landlord flat above. As she left her car and walked into the now deserted and silent car park the 3 floodlights which covered the entire area switched off leaving them glowing eerily in the dark. Mary used the darkness to check the security; there were 2 CCTU cameras, one on the front of the building covering the entrance the other at the rear of the car park. Walking to the one in the car park she was excited to see the power cable to the camera ran straight up the pole from the junction box mounted on it – easy out!

CHAPTER 64

IT WAS FRIDAY THE 15th and Mary prepared herself very carefully; frizzy black wig, heavy make-up, blue contact lenses, tight jeans, cropped top and completed with a second hand leather jacket she had purchased from the op shop.

At 9:00pm she drove herself to The Dragon and parked 100 metres down the road. Leaving her car she proceeded from the road to the garden bed at the rear of the pub. Keeping behind the bushes she made her way to the pole with the camera. Taking a pair of wire cutters from the leather jacket she cut the coaxial cable that led to the camera. Apart from the motorbikes, the car park was empty.

She opened the bar door, the room was full of skimpily dressed girls with bikies leering after them. Scoping the room she did not see him at first but there was Tex, sitting at the bar with the same girl again. She made her way through them all to the stool next to Tex and sat down. He had noticed her coming over and was studying her intently when it slowly dawned on him who she was. Despite her inner self loathing him with every fibre of her being, she smiled a seductive smile. He turned to the girl beside him "Fuck off," he said "go on, fuck off." She looked at Mary, without recognition, slid off the bar stool and wandered away.

"So," he leered, "you couldn't keep away from me." The thought of having sex across two generations powered his drive and his pants bulged as he savoured the thought. He turned to the barman and shouted "Jack, two pints." He lit a cigarette using a gold American Zippo lighter and watched the wick burn a little before closing the lid and turning his attention back to Mary.

Over the next hour Tex had devoured three pints while Mary listened to his continuing repulsive dialogue. Fortunately for her the bar was full of empty glasses and she was able to pour away most of the pints he thought she had drunk. "You are quite a woman." he said looking over her quizzically, "but why the disguise?"

"I didn't want to be recognised, you have a quite the reputation you know."

He laughed loudly "You're right." he said. "Save me place, I'm going for a piss."

It was close to 11:00pm and the time was right, half the bikies had left the pub with only a few remaining. Being sure that she wasn't being watched, she removed the Rohypnol from her bag and slipped them into his almost full pint glass and waited for his return. She didn't have to wait long; a few minutes after his return the last of the bikies pushed open the door and shouted "See ya." as he left the bar. Tex downed his beer in one go.

The drug had started to work quickly and soon Tex began to slur his speech, "Come on, let's go fuck." he said. Standing uncertainly and leaning heavily on Mary, they staggered out into the car park where he became almost instantly comatose. Struggling, she guided him to the only bike left in the car park. As she anticipated, the car park was now deserted. He slumped toward the ground as she manoeuvred him so that he sat with his back against the bike, feet out in front of him and his head lolled forward. He was out cold.

The difficult part done, Mary took his cigarettes out of his top pocket placing one in his mouth and scattering the rest over the ground around him. Pulling off the petrol hose that leads from the tank to the carburettor, she turned on the fuel tap and ran the petrol all over Tex. She grabbed the helmet that was sitting on his seat, held it under the stream of petrol, and then placed it on his head. Returning the hose to its place, she looked around her but all was quiet; just the dripping of the petrol, the fumes filling her nostrils. She flicked the wheel and the blue flame sprang to life, running around the wind shield and flickered. "For Helen." she mouthed as she dropped the lighter into his lap. The flames danced around his spreadeagled body,

Without a backward glance Mary sprinted to her car and as she opened the door she heard the whoosh as the tank blew. She started the car and watched the flames briefly before driving away.

The next day Mary placed the wig, clothes and contact lens in a plastic bag to take to work. Once there she would place it all in the incinerator for waste disposal where it would be burnt and disappear up the waste chimney.

* * * * * * * * * * * * * * *

Malcolm tipped the contents of the brown envelope onto his desk; a lighter, a charred wallet with melted credit cards, and a driver's licence – Terrance Anthony Anderson - no loss to society he thought. He picked up the blackened lighter *To V,*

All my love, S. was engraved on the back. He placed all the items back in the envelope and closed the file, placing them both in the wire basket on his desk. His report read *Accidental death by fire caused by a petrol leak ignited when lighting a cigarette. No further action required.*

CHAPTER 65

THE PILOT CHECKED THE INSTRUMENTS carefully before taxiing to the far end of the runway, turning he lined up the little two seater plane. They were on their way. At 60knots he gently pulled back the wheel and the plane floated off the ground into the air. Banking over, he headed into the sun. Clyde looked down at the little colourful settlement in the desert at the foot of the mountains. A group of people were waving and he could see the arena and the flags hanging limp in the morning stillness. The plane jumped and bucked as it gained height, riding the hot air currents already rising from the desert sand. Clyde closed his eyes and tried to force his thoughts to his task. He was having a great deal of difficulty in concentrating.

Arriving at Gatwick Clyde was drained. The adrenalin from the games had long since left him leaving him filled with mixed emotions; a deep felt sense of achieving little with regard to his quest to avenge Vanessa and the loss of Adel's company. Putting these thoughts to the back of his mind, he concentrated on his next step. He went to the coffee bar and made a call. Patrick picked up the phone, "Hello." he said before listening intently to Clyde. "OK son," he finally said, "I'll find out what I can, call me back at 3:00pm."

Clyde phoned at exactly 3pm. "Well here's the news son, Sean McCracken caught the boat back across the water today and will arrive in Dublin at 6:15pm. He's not under surveillance by our people in Ireland. They left him at Liverpool as he boarded the ferry." Clyde, be very careful, he will be on his guard after Libya."

"Thanks Pat." Clyde said and closed the call. He sat back in his chair and closed his eyes. The coffee bar was full of people and the chattering and droning of people's voices slowly subsided as he went back over the past few weeks. It was fate which had prevented him from ending his quest to avenge his sister's murder but it was also fate that had crossed his path with Adel. He thought about her now and could smell the Jasmine and taste her lips, the essence of her returning to his mind made him smile to himself. With an effort he pulled himself back to his surroundings determined to finish what he had started and return to Libya for his Adel. He would resign his commission if necessary to be with her. The decision made, he finished his coffee and stood to leave.

Clyde was aware he looked every inch an SAS Colonel, tall muscular with short cropped hair, wide shoulders and a lean body. As he turned to leave, he noticed a man and a woman at a table in the corner of the coffee bar, the man was staring intently at him and did not waiver his stare as Clyde looked directly at him. He smiled at Clyde and Clyde approached the table. "Do I know you?" Clyde asked.

The woman smiled "No, but we know you. Even without a description we knew it was you, as you are who you are Colonel. Patrick told us you would be here."

Puzzled, Clyde sat at their table. "Ok so you know who I am. Now, who are you?"

The man held out his hand. "Jack O'Reilly and Mary Donovan." Clyde shook the offered hand satisfied that Patrick had indeed informed them who he was. The hand was dry and powerful with a vibrancy that comes from strong arms and shoulders.

"We are with the Ulster constabulary, the secret service, the Irish equivalent of M16. We have no jurisdiction outside Ireland but we have ears in many places. The Libya connection we know about, your involvement we do not have clear knowledge of be suspect we have the same objectives. Your objectives we understand to be personal, but in many ways they mirror our own objectives. We are civilians, you are military, in a branch which are the best at counter insurgence."

"We have tabs on your man, Sean McCracken, and at present he is in Ireland heading south. He has contacted or been contacted by no-one in the 'Sons of Erin' which is strange. He was born and raised in Ballihorrie in Southern Ireland and we suspect that is where he is heading. He is an extremely dangerous man that we have been unable to catch in anything illegal; and believe me we have tried. I'm sure you are aware just how sharp and cunning this man is, truly smart and slippery. However, several small changes lead us to believe that Libya did something to him and we think he is going back to his roots at Ballihorrie."

Clyde studied both the man and woman in turn, each of them holding his eyes without a trace of falsehood. He felt he could trust the information he had just received. Clyde stood, shook their hands in turn, first the man and then the woman. The woman held Clyde's hand a little longer than was necessary and pulled him closer to him. "He has killed a lot of innocent people," she whispered. "far, far too many" Her lips tightened as she spoke. "Make it so and good luck to you."

Strangely, airport security at Dublin did not x-ray luggage and Clyde picked up his carry-all at the luggage elevator and walked through with nothing to declare. The bag in fact contained his Arab bow and the last arrow. He noticed a customs officer, a smart looking blonde woman, looking intently at him and as he passed her she said "Could you step this way please sir?" and motioned him to a nearby bench. "Could you open your backpack for me please sir?" Pausing, Clyde looked around the terminal and noticed Mary waiting at the car hire counter. Catching her eye, he beckoned her over. The customs officer was clearly impressed when Mary took her to one side and showed her her warrant card. Clyde could see on the card the anti-terrorist stamp of the Secret Service department. Mary turned to Clyde, winked and waved him away.

Clyde left the airport and walked onto the concourse looking for a taxi. He was approached by a man asking "Are you Clyde Machin?" When Clyde nodded the man handed him a set of keys and said "It is a red Hyundai Excel parked in the car park, row 2, number 48, compliments of Mr Patrick. When you are done with the car, leave the keys under the seat and lock the door, we will use our own set of keys to retrieve the car."

CHAPTER 66

SEAN, AFTER MAKING HIS WAY home again, now sat on the elm chair at the kitchen table of his Aunt's farmhouse and looked around the room reflecting that nothing had changed in 100 years. His Aunt took the blackened kettle off the fire and filled the brown teapot. She sat with him and poured the tea into 2 chipped mugs, from a large white jug she poured milk into the strong brown tea and sighed.

"Oh Sean, I told them who you were," she said sadly, "but it made no difference. They took him out into the fold and shot him in the head."

Sean placed his hand on her weathered arm, "I know," he said, "they are both now dead."

She looked up at him with tears in her eyes, her old lined face full of sorrow. "But that hasn't helped at all."

Sean sat a while longer with his Aunt before rising and saying "I have to go. I've left you a package in the bedroom." He bent and kissed her forehead.

On his own again, Sean made a phone call to Father Kelly, "Hello." he answered.

"Hello Father, this is Sean McCracken."

"Sean McCracken." he replied. "Well, I haven't heard that name in a long time."

"I know Father, I would like for you to take my confession."

"It must be 20 years since I took your last confession, are you OK?"

"I know Father, a lifetime. I'm tired and I need you to give me absolution. I have a great black cloud hanging over me and it is spreading."

"My son, I can be at the church in an hour. I can meet you then."

"Thank you Father, I will see you there."

"Are you sure you can find your way to the church after all this time?" Father Kelly asked good humouredly.

Sean laughed a thunderous laugh. "I think so Father, I think so."

* * * * * * * * * * * * * *

Clyde had never been to Ballihorrie but he knew Southern Ireland well enough to know that he would stand out like a sore thumb. He had to make an effort to blend more readily. From an Oxfam shop in Dublin he bought a jacket and trousers and a non-descript hat. Then he went to an engineering supply shop where he purchased a surveyors staff. With this in the back of his car he set off to the south coast.

* * * * * * * * * * * * * *

Father Kelly was quite old and frail now and sat hunched over in the confessional straining to hear Sean's voice. "Forgive me Father for I have sinned."

"How long since your last confession?" Father Kelly automatically replied.

"Many a year Father, perhaps too long." Sean replied.

"Tell me your troubles son."

"They are enormous and many Father but one in particular weighs heavier than others; I need to repent this most recent of my crimes. I.........I.........killed a retarded girl."

"Oh Sean. Not your sister?"

"No Father but a very similar girl. Oh, please God forgive me."

"Are you truly sorry for this sin my son?"

"Yes Father, I am."

* * * * * * * * * * * * * *

Clyde had parked behind the old Yew trees and the side of the church. Earlier he had noted an old priest walk out of the manse and up the churchyard into the church. Taking out a flask and a packet of sandwiches, Clyde placed them on the bonnet of the car as if he had stopped for a snack. He put together the bow and knocked an arrow into the string. He went around to the boot and placed the bow and arrow inside while he continued watching the church.

A green Toyota pulled up in the church car park and through the trees Clyde could see the driver was a tall muscular man of about 30 years of age. Finally, it appeared the time had come.

Clyde's car was well hidden and he did not think the man took any notice of him as he walked into the church. The churchyard was completely deserted and the trees shielded the church from the nearest houses. Clyde pushed the old wooden door open, surprisingly it made no sound as it swung open enough to allow him to go inside. It was dark and gloomy inside and he could hear murmuring coming from the confessional booth which was closed by a curtain on rings. He could see a foot with a leather boot without a sole poking out of the side of the booth.

Placing the release catch around the string, Clyde drew back the arrow as the hand holding the catch touched his cheek, the string touched his lips and he felt his heartbeat as he calculated where the chest area would be behind the closed curtain. 'Thrum' the arrow left the bow at 120 foot pounds of energy, vibrating on its path and disappeared through the curtain.

* * * * * * * * * * * * * *

Although this was an unusual confession Father Kelly, who had heard thousands of confessions in his time, was operating on auto-pilot and was still aware of the rest of his surroundings. He heard a sold thump that he had not been able to identify and now there was another noise, drip, drip, drip.

The arrow had entered Sean's chest just below his right arm and passed out of the left side of his chest at the front slumping him forward. His head was touching the timber sill, his life blood running down the shaft and pooling on the floor. By the time the priest pulled back the curtain, the Hyundai was miles away.

There was of course a police investigation but the only evidence was an ancient arrow that could not be identified. Nobody had noticed the Red Hyundai or any persons hanging around the church.

Word filtered back to Dublin and Jack O'Reilly and Mary Donovan high fived each other, unable to contain their grins.

CHAPTER 67

Bernard sat well down in the car seat. It was parked in a lay by across the road from the Henderson's. The car was not conspicuous as it was parked amongst another three cars which were all empty. He took a deep drag of the joint and sucked in a lung full of the musty smoke. Holding it in for a full 10 seconds he exhaled slowly, the blue grey smoke curled round the brown sun visor. The drug was absorbed into his blood through the lung walls. In his brain, his senses sharpened.

The motorbike roared around the corner; Bernard sank lower in his seat. The bike slowed into the lay by, there were two people on it; a bikie in leathers and chains with a girl as pillion, neither were wearing a helmet. Bernard checked his watch it was 11:30pm. They had parked about 10metres away and at first he had wished they would move one but soon it was clear that he was in for some entertainment.

He heard the girl say "No, not tonight, I came on this morning." The man was clearly angry and pushed her violently and she fell onto the gravel. At first Bernard thought the man was going to kick her but he changed his mind and got back on the bike, kicking it to life. "Terry," the girl said. "Terry." The bikie ignored her as he revved the big bike and roared off back towards town.

Bernard looked at the attractive girl with long dark hair. She had got back to her feet now and stood watching the red tail lights of the rapidly disappearing motorbike. He took a long drag of the joint and flicked it out of the window. Opening the door of the car he stepped out onto the gravel, "Well, well." he said. "Left you to walk home hey?" With a leer he walked towards Helen Johnson.

CHAPTER 68

A LGERNON HAD BEEN FEELING VERY run down; the business of Bernard's death had caused him a great deal of trouble. When the doctor had suggested a check up he had at first been inclined to say no. However, he was nearly fifty years old; perhaps he should, just in case.

He sat stunned, again he stared at the report – HIV Positive – he had been summoned to Head Office.

Mad Coxy had been the unknown cause at Wakefield Jail as he pounded away the small broken blood vessels in Bernard's anus spreading blood and mucus along his penis. The spurt of grey semen spread the deadly virus into this soup of mucus and blood.

CHAPTER 69

SEAN MCCRACKEN HAD PAID THE price. He had died as he had lived – violently - in the few seconds before the massive hemorrhaging wound sucked out his life. He desperately sought absolution, knowing full well that his soul would rot in the eternal fires of hell. Ironically the events which had culminated in his execution should not have brought it about. As he died, the events were lost with him..........

On April the fifteenth, a Friday night, Sean's nondescript car waited at the traffic lights on the corner of main street when suddenly the door opened and a lumpy female climbed into the passengers seat. For a moment Sean looked at the face, a grinning idiot face of a Mongol. She closed the door behind her and Sean could smell the ammoniac stench of urine soaked under clothes. He was about to shout at her to get out – the shout died in his throat. He lost control and let out the clutch with a jerk and accelerated away. The girl carried on grinning when suddenly he slammed on the brakes and the girls head crashed into the dash with a thud. She cried out in pain. All the years he had suffered the humiliation at home consumed him in a fury, he beat the face to a pulp. He kept going long after she was dead – thumping, smashing and beating all the hate and frustration washing over him in waves.

As quickly as he had started, he stopped and slumped back in his seat, exhausted and panting like a marathon runner. He checked over his shoulder down Canal Road, it was empty. He leant over the crumpled body and opened the door pushing her out onto the curb. Closing the door he drove away, the urine soaked seat causing him to gag and retch.

HARRY

On Friday the 21st a blue letter arrived in Charlie's letter box.....

www.ingramcontent.com/pod-product-compliance
Lightning Source LLC
Chambersburg PA
CBHW030823210726
48290CB00002B/733